Summer Escapes

Can you take the heat?

Love is in the air and the forecasts have promised a spell of sun, sea and sizzling romance. So let us whisk you away to this season's most glamorous destinations full of rolling hills, blissful beaches and piping hot passion! Take your seat and follow as these sun-kissed couples find their forever on faraway shores. After all, it's been said you should catch flights, not feelings—but who says you can't do both?

Start your journey to true love in...

The Venice Reunion Arrangement
by Michelle Douglas

Dating Game with Her Enemy
by Justine Lewis

The Billionaire She Loves to Hate
by Scarlett Clarke

Cinderella's Greek Island Temptation
by Cara Colter

A Reunion in Tuscany
by Sophie Pembroke

Their Mauritius Wedding Ruse
by Nina Milne

Available now!

And look out for the next stop of your travels with...

Fake Date on the Orient Express
by Jessica Gilmore

Coming soon!

Dear Reader,

Many, many years ago, I had taken a love for writing and turned it into a diploma in journalism. However, after graduating from that program, I made the startling and somewhat disheartening discovery that I didn't like journalism!

As so often is the way, the right thing happened at the right time. For me, it was seeing an interview with a woman from my hometown who was writing for Harlequin. Something inside of me whispered, with absolute certainty, *that's it*. (Judith Duncan, I am forever grateful for that serendipitous moment when I saw you on television.)

The first effort I submitted was set in Greece, a popular romance destination at the time. It was gently refused, with the suggestion that maybe I should use a setting I was more familiar with. And I did. My second effort was accepted and I have never looked back.

Now, setting this book in Greece is a full circle moment for me. I hope you enjoy getting to know Gage and Hailey against this beautiful backdrop!

With best wishes,

Cara Colter

CINDERELLA'S GREEK ISLAND TEMPTATION

CARA COLTER

Recycling programs for this product may not exist in your area.

ISBN-13: 978-1-335-21645-8

Cinderella's Greek Island Temptation

For questions and comments about the quality of this book, please contact us at CustomerService@Harlequin.com.

Harlequin Enterprises ULC
22 Adelaide St. West, 41st Floor
Toronto, Ontario M5H 4E3, Canada
www.Harlequin.com

Printed in U.S.A.

Cara Colter shares her home in beautiful British Columbia, Canada, with her husband of more than thirty years, an ancient crabby cat and several horses. She has three grown children and two grandsons.

Books by Cara Colter

Harlequin Romance

A White Christmas in Whistler

The Billionaire's Festive Reunion

Blossom and Bliss Weddings

Second Chance Hawaiian Honeymoon
Hawaiian Nights with the Best Man

Fairy Tales in Maine

Invitation to His Billion-Dollar Ball

Winter Escapes

Their Hawaiian Marriage Reunion

Matchmaker and the Manhattan Millionaire
His Cinderella Next Door
The Wedding Planner's Christmas Wish
Snowbound with the Prince
Bahamas Escape with the Best Man
Snowed In with the Billionaire
Winning Over the Brooding Billionaire
Accidentally Engaged to the Billionaire

Visit the Author Profile page
at Harlequin.com for more titles.

To Lynne Cormack

With deep appreciation for friendships
that stand the test of time.

Praise for
Cara Colter

"Ms. Colter's writing style is one you will
want to continue to read. Her descriptions
place you there.... This story does have a HEA
but leaves you wanting more."
—*Harlequin Junkie* on *His Convenient Royal Bride*

CHAPTER ONE

GAGE PAYTON FLOATED ALONE. He was flat on his back, his arms spread wide to the world, in the inky darkness of the Aegean Sea. He was gloriously sandwiched between balmy summer night air and warm, salty water. His every sense felt awake and alive.

It was the first time in a very long time he had felt like this.

Relaxed. At ease. Free.

He felt somehow connected to the swirl of stars above him and the water that held him.

Gone, finally, was that nagging feeling of that indefinable *something* missing. It had been a good decision to take a break on his superyacht, *Seas du Jour,* which was now moored off the Greek island of Crete.

He congratulated himself on living out the promise of the vessel's name. Seizing the moment, the day. Carpe diem.

How could anything be missing from his life, anyway? He was the poster child for *arrival.* The one-hundred-and-twenty-foot fully crewed yacht bobbing comfortably at anchor just a few feet from him was a testimony to that. Wasn't it?

He was annoyed with himself. That single thought—the crazy longing for *something more* when he was the man who had everything—had intruded on his moment of perfect tranquility.

Gage took a deep breath, let the thoughts drift away and allowed himself to sink deeper into the sensation of the sea holding him, of not needing to do or be anything.

Ah, there it was, again. Utter stillness.

But, really? If anyone knew that serenity as a permanent state was as unattainable as arriving at an oasis mirage shimmering on a desert horizon, it should be him. He was twenty-nine years old, and the adrenaline-filled career he had loved most—playing professional American football—was over.

Eighteen months ago, after yet another concussion, Gage had been warned that one more blow to the head could cause irreversible damage to the brain or possibly death. Though he had not had a single symptom of CTE—chronic traumatic encephalopathy—even he wasn't stubborn enough, or enough of a gambler, to put the doc's dire warning to the test.

It didn't matter that his business enterprise, Touchdown, along with his football earnings, had skyrocketed him into the realm of billionaires. It didn't matter that he had applied the same grit, determination and sweat equity that had once made him America's hero in the football world to achieve heady successes in other fields.

There was an emptiness in him that football had once filled.

Before football he didn't recall any sense of emptiness. And before football he certainly didn't have to run every single encounter through the filter of *What do they want from me and what kind of treachery are they capable of to get it?*

Sometimes, he found himself longing for the simple days and dreams of his youth before fame and fortune had called his name.

Gage frowned. He realized it wasn't *thoughts*—as annoying as they were—pulling him away from the brief feeling he'd had of being a part of the stars and the sea, with no line of separation between them. Not this time.

No, it was a sound that was intruding on his pursuit of tranquility.

He listened, straining his ears. The call of a bird? Were there birds that hunted the waters here at night? He wasn't familiar enough with the Greek islands to know.

He heard nothing, and tried to make himself relax again. But no, the moment was gone. He righted himself in the water and trod steadily. He glanced toward the yacht to see if anyone else had heard anything. Its sleek lines gorgeous, the yacht had its nighttime running lights on, but it was past midnight, and all but the night crew would have retired.

Squinting across the water, Gage could make out the Venetian lighthouse, its silhouette blacker than the night sky, the strobe winking at him.He could also see the illumination from the charming historical city of Chania reflected on the water, whimsical and blurry, like a Monet painting.

He turned and took a single stroke toward the lower aft deck of the yacht, the "beach" platform used for getting on and off or to enter and exit the water for swimming and water games, but then he heard it again. He froze, mid stroke.

Not a bird.

More like the mew of a newly born kitten searching blindly for its mother. It felt as if his head was beginning to hurt from listening so hard.

Gone completely was the serenity of moments ago. Instead, he could feel himself tensing, *ready.* Peripherally, he welcomed the old feeling of adrenaline beginning to pump through his veins.

And then, there it was, a bare whisper on the breeze. There was no mistaking it this time.

"Help..."

The adrenaline surged. Shore was too far away for the sound to have come from there. Someone was in that dark water with him, and the last thing they were feeling was serenity.

"Hey," he yelled. "Is there someone in the water?"

Silence.

"Hey," he called again. "Where are you?"

On the deck above the beach platform, he saw Seth Wesley separate himself from the shadows.

Gage hadn't known he was there, but he should have. Seth took his job—protection specialist aka bodyguard—very seriously.

Seth was from before: before a million-dollar contract right out of college had catapulted Gage into a world no ordinary person could ever prepare themselves for. Nothing about his solid middle-class upbringing had made him ready for *that*: money, attention, fame, adulation.

Betrayal.

He and Seth had been best buddies all through high school. They'd played sports together and spent their summers lifeguarding and meeting girls at the local pool. But then their paths parted, both of them moving toward their destinies. Gage to the university football scholarship and the professional athlete career, and Seth to disappear into a world that, in retrospect, he'd been born to as much as Gage had been born to competition.

Seth had gone to the navy and then SEALs and then something secretive and shadowy that had somehow resulted in his leg nearly being blown off.

They'd always kept in touch and Seth had been one of the first investors in Gage's company, Touchdown, but it was the wounds of forced retirements from careers they both loved most that had brought the childhood friends back together.

An escalation of intrusions into his private life, and a final shocking act of duplicity at the hands of someone he had trusted, had made Gage realize that, as much as he longed for it, there would be no *normal* for him again, ever.

He could not go grab a case of beer from the corner store.

He could not make an impulsive decision to attend a high school or college football game.

He could not go to a restaurant.

He could not step out the door of any of his three Stateside houses without being photographed, followed, harassed.

He could not even go visit his mom and dad, or his sister and brother-in-law, his two rambunctious nephews and his fairy tale-obsessed niece, in their sleepy small hometown in Iowa without turning their lives into a media circus.

He could not just find a hometown girl, get married, settle down, have kids and have the kind of life he had grown up with. He hadn't even realized that scenario had even been somewhere in the back of his mind until he'd realized he couldn't have it.

And all those realizations had come *before* his freshest lesson: even people he had given his rare trust to could sell him out if the price was right.

He'd bought the yacht after *Wheeple Magazine*, in a move that was notorious and unauthorized, had devoted the entire issue to "Gage Payton: Catch of the Century," as if he was a bloody fish to be hooked.

Unfortunately, the facts had not been nearly salacious enough. A man who had a secret penchant for peanut butter and onion sandwiches and used his luscious private home theater almost exclusively for an endless loop of the 1979 Super Bowl XIII, Steelers vs. Cowboys, did not magazines sell. What sold was innuendo and half-truths, the suggestion that his bedroom had a revolving door on it. The story claimed that, in a three-month period alone, he'd entertained a redheaded film star, a raven-haired songstress and a certain princess bad girl.

Gage's sister, Kate, after reading the issue cover to cover had slammed it down, and exclaimed, "'Catch of the Century'? This presents you as a heartless player! What self-respecting woman would want you after this?"

And then she'd sighed heavily, because she felt quite free to weigh in disapprovingly on his choices about who he spent his time with, and she probably had long since given up on any self-respecting woman ever wanting him anyway.

But to Gage, the real hurt and humiliation had come from discovering who the source of the article was— a traitor within his trusted inner circle.

It had crushed him that it was Babba, a woman from his hometown whom he had known since he was a kid, and to whom he had given the opportunity of a lifetime by selecting her to run his kitchen and his household.

She'd been with him for years, practically from the beginning. It was like having a grandmother in residence. She'd risen to the challenge, going from cooking perogies to making herself an expert on the dietary requirements of an elite athlete.

He'd treated her—as he liked to think he treated everyone—with respect and genuine liking. He'd appreciated her. He'd given her bonuses. He'd sent her on trips. He'd bought Christmas presents for her grandkids.

One of those grandkids, Karl, was a problem child. While Gage was quite willing to help Babba's family with private tuition, an unexpected vehicle repair or even a down payment for a house, he'd drawn the line at Sammy's ongoing legal problems and Babba would have certainly known better than to approach him about needing money owed to drug dealers. So, she'd got the money another way.

Still, she was the person he'd least guarded himself against, least suspected of sneakily recording things he'd said or the people who had visited his home, least suspected of taking covert pictures of him.

The photos she'd supplied to the magazine had been utterly cringeworthy.

Gage emerging from the bathroom with a towel cinched around his waist, hefting himself out of the pool or coming, sweat-covered, from the weight room. Those photos made it look as if he spent his every waking hour wandering around his house barely dressed and always ready for encounters of the amorous kind.

When he'd confronted Babba about the complete invasion of his privacy and asked why she had chosen those particular pictures and lied to the magazine about him having affairs with women who were just acquaintances, she'd said, with a shocking lack of repentance, "Sex sells."

He had, of course, contemplated taking legal action against both Babba and the magazine, but a very good lawyer had told him if he wanted even *more* attention and to prolong the pain and humiliation of having his private life exposed, a lawsuit would be the best way to do that. Instead, he'd fired Babba and his attorney had drafted NDA agreements that every single person in his employ had to sign.

Then, he'd bought a yacht. He didn't like to think of it as going into hiding. It was more a need to protect his privacy, to get his sense of sanctuary back. Still, even now, though the entire crew were ex-navy, hand-picked by Seth—men and women who knew how to keep things to themselves—Gage sometimes could not get over the creepy residue of Babba's betrayal: a sensation of being watched.

But at least the yacht gave Gage a place where he could meet his family and friends without intrusions. He had the NDAs and had also developed a set of strict rules around the use of cell phones on board, which his family ribbed him about, but still respected.

He was also finding out, with gratitude, that he was less well-known in other parts of the world than in the United States, and many countries weren't as celebrity-obsessed. Sometimes, he could experience tiny tastes of normal life.

Was that what that longing was for, especially

after Babba? The one thing he could not have? A normal life?

Seth had been working on giving him his life back—inasmuch as he could get it back. He became Gage's right-hand man, and though he was extremely skilled and took the job very seriously, the relationship was not so much one of employer to employee as one of deep friendship based on mutual respect and trust.

It was Seth who'd encouraged Gage to master the art not so much of disguise, as blending in. His hair was naturally curly, part of a diverse ethnic heritage on his mother's side that included Asian, African and Native American. Keeping it close-cropped had been conducive with his lifestyle in sports.

But now, he had for the first time in his life grown a beard, and his hair brushed along the nape of his neck. The *new* look, along with a ball cap and mirrored sunglasses that hid his rather distinctive eyes, made Gage Payton look like 90 percent of all men in his age group. He did not think his own mother would have paused if she passed him on the street.

Yesterday, he and Seth had taken the dinghy in—not the attention-drawing helicopter—and actually walked down a cobblestone street in Chania, stopping at a little café. They had not garnered one single second look.

"What's up, boss?" Seth called now from the deck.

"I don't know for sure. I thought I heard something."

Seth cocked his head, listening.

And then they both heard it again. A feminine voice, out there in that sea of endless black.

Muted by distance, but still, the terror came through in that single word.

"Help..."

CHAPTER TWO

WAS THAT CRY weaker than it had been when Gage had first heard it? Farther away?

"I hear you," Gage called, as loudly as he could. His voice had a booming quality. And then, to Seth, he said, "Jet Ski?"

"We won't hear her calling over the engine. And it's too dark. There's a serious risk of running her over if we take a Jet Ski."

Gage made his decision. He called out, loudly, "I'm coming. Keep calling, so that I can find you."

Out of the corner of his eye, he saw his friend race over the darkened main deck and throw on a spotlight that began to sweep the waters. The beam glanced off something and Gage felt his focus and readiness peak.

It could have been a buoy, but it also could have been a head bobbing in the black water. He heard Seth hit the water, not even hesitating to dive off the second floor of the boat.

Go time.

Though he had not played football for eighteen months, two weeks and six days, his fitness regime was as much a part of him as breathing. Even given his physical conditioning, Gage's breath came hard and his muscles screamed as a sense of urgency propelled him through the water with as much power as he could summon.

The resolve, the sense of mission, felt like a homecoming, as if he'd fallen back into himself after wandering away for a while.

He was aware that Seth was also swimming hard, somewhere behind him.

Gage stopped, briefly, recalibrating, listening.

"Let me know where you are," he shouted.

Seth, fully clothed, caught up to him. Despite the boat's searchlight, and the beam from the lighthouse, the seaaround them seemed mostly dark, empty and endless. Gage's breathing was loud and ragged against the absolute quiet of the night.

"Do you see anything?" he asked Seth desperately, as the other man drew closer. "Hear anything?"

They both trod water, straining their eyes and ears.

Nothing.

And then came the faintest of splashing sounds.

"Yell," Gage commanded. "Help us find you."

"Here. I'm here." A distinct voice, but weak. It occurred to him whoever was in those Greek waters was speaking English with what he thought was a British accent.

"Keep calling."

Silence, and then, "Marco."

The age-old game of following a voice to find someone.

"Polo!" he yelled, letting her know he heard, he understood.

It came again. A little stronger? "Marco."

He zeroed in on it. "Keep doing that!"

Gage had thought he was at max effort until he headed toward that voice. Then he really put on the jets. He finally spotted the woman or maybe a girl.

He was shocked to find he had a burst of strength left and he closed the remaining distance between them with a head-up freestyle that took him to her in less than a second.

At first he thought she was wearing a black bathing cap, but then he saw it was her short, short hair plastered to her skull, like otter fur. Her face was a white moon of terror against that endless black backdrop, and it was immediately obvious, despite her delicate features, that she was not a child.

Gage knew all the rules of lifesaving. He'd been a lifeguard at the outdoor pool in his hometown since he was fifteen. Even if he hadn't done it for years, the chain of rescue was burned into his brain.

So he knew the correct order of actions and the absolute importance of it.

It was like going up the rungs of a ladder: Don't get too close; talk first; assess the situation; keep the victim calm; see if she can follow instructions. It was only after going through the initial checklist unsuccessfully that he should reach out to her with something—not that he had anything. Body contact was supposed to be the very last resort.

His head knew all those things, but his heart told him something just as important and it was completely different and against all the rules.

Finally, she could see him. Hailey watched, her arms and legs wind milling wildly, but with less and less strength, as the swimmer moved powerfully toward her.

The exhaustion that had nearly done her in gave way to exhilaration.

It was real. The voice had been real; the man coming toward her was real.

She was aware that it was nothing short of a miracle. Just as she had resigned herself to the inevitability of a watery death, someone had heard her. She was going to be rescued.

"Marco," she called, even though it was now clear he had already pinpointed her location in all this black water.

Her sense of relief and joy intensified as she realized there were two people swimming toward her—that it was not a lone person out here with her, responsible for plucking her from this dark abyss that she had been certain was going to kill her.

Her relief was tempered with slight chagrin when the swimmer farther away from her started calling instructions to the man closest.

"Don't make contact. She'll pull you down. Get

her to roll over. Here, I'm taking off my shirt. Use that to reach her."

Rationally, she knew the second rescuer was putting safety first, but irrationally she wanted—no, needed—contact *right now.*

Thankfully, the closer man ignored the instructions, coming toward her without hesitation, closing the remaining distance between them with speed and ease.

And then he was there, right in front of her.

Despite her situation—or maybe because of it—her awareness seemed unusually heightened. Hailey took in the water sluicing down the chiseled masculine perfection of his nose and the bearded cheekbones and chin. She considered maybe this was, after all, a dream of rescue, fabricated by an exhausted mind, rather than the real thing, because surely no mortal man this gorgeous could just rise out of the sea in front of her?

His eyes were burning with the fierce determination of a warrior, someone who scoffed at death as if it were a puny thing, insubstantial in the face of his will.

Her tired mind grappled with what was right in front of her, focusing deeply on him, taking in every detail as proof she was not making him up. Who, beyond a great artist, Michelangelo for instance, could conjure this?

Those remarkable eyes were thickly fringed with lashes that were crusted with drops of water, as was the beard that framed his lips, the lower one plump, with the faintest line down the middle of it. Tangled, soaked hair, some shade of dark, the same as his beard, curled wildly around the column of a powerful neck and fell to broad shoulders.

But in the end, it felt as if there was only one way to convince her despairing mind that he was not a complete figment of her imagination. She did exactly what the second man had warned against.

She flung herself at her rescuer, curling her arms around that strong neck to pull herself yet closer.

She was not sure she had ever experienced such intense relief as when she pressed herself into the hard length of his body. Feeling his arms close around her, the press of his water-slick skin against her sodden dress, was pure bliss.

He was real. In fact, he was about the realest thing Hailey had ever felt.

His sinewy strength was abundantly apparent. In fact, he took her weight easily, his arms coming underneath her own, then knotting at the small of her back.

She wanted nothing more than to give herself over to him completely, knowing she had not an ounce of energy left, but it was as if a red warning light was blinking on and off in her brain.

Danger. Danger. Danger.

She contemplated that, confused. Wasn't she *out* of danger?

Yes, yes, she was. So, Hailey shamelessly pulled her body tighter into the man's, sucked into him like a limpet clinging fiercely to a rock being bashed by waves. It was when she felt his heat radiating ever so subtly through the cold water that she became aware how very chilled she was. Her teeth began to chatter.

Again, she was aware of her highly heightened senses. She took in, with grave gratitude, all the evidence of him being solid and tangible. Hailey could feel the steady beat of her rescuer's heart. She could feel the broadness of his chest, the jut of his ribcage, the hollow of his belly, the powerful thrust of his legs holding them both above water.

She did not feel it in the way a woman is aware of a man, but in the way of someone who had looked death in the face and was clinging tightly to her second chance.

She was suddenly able to define the brilliance she had seen sparking in his eyes. He was the life force.

So why was that red light in her mind still blinking, way off in the distance, as if she was approaching a train track, urging caution?

"Don't let her pull you under," the other man warned him. "Let me take her."

But her rescuer did not release her.

"She doesn't pose any danger to me," he said, and the pure graveled strength of his voice reassured her, again, this was real. "You don't have anything left, do you, darling?"

There was that word again. *Danger.* Of course she did not pose any danger to him! And what possible danger could he pose to her?

He was *saving* her.

She nodded slightly against his chest. She realized he had an accent. American? That sweet, slow drawl, *darling*, curled around her, like smoke promising the warmth of a fire.

"I don't know what you're wearing," he said, "but it's tangling in my legs. It's dragging us both down, like an anchor."

"It's a dress. I tried to take it off," she stammered. "It was pulling me down. But every time I tried, my head would go under water."

"It's okay," he said, keeping her distress at bay, "Do you want it off?"

He could not know how much she wanted to be rid of that wet weight, the drag on her exhausted limbs.

But still, she had to think about it, as if her brain was working way too slow. Her brain was stuck on the danger signal. She overrode the message it was sending her.

"Yes."

But having made the decision to remove the dress, the distress returned like water that had been building pressure behind a dam. Her heart went crazy.

Something tried to push through the fog in her mind, some kind of memory, sepia-toned and elusive.

A man. She couldn't quite see him. It was only a feeling. Of laughter. Of connection. And then of something else. Dark. Was it fury? Hers or his?

"I've changed my mind. I'll leave the dress on," she said, with as much firmness as she could manage with her heavy limbs, numb skin and chattering teeth.

"Hey," he said, cocking his head at her, as if he could sense that fury and distress she didn't quite understand. "Of course, whatever you're comfortable with."

The reassurance quieted something in her that had tried to rear up, ugly. Her rational mind kicked in.

Hailey loosened one hand from around his neck, yanked at one shoulder strap and then the other, then squirmed against him. He realized what she was doing and also freed one hand. He grabbed at the hem of the dress and yanked it down. For one moment she panicked—was it because the dress felt as if it was going to wrap around both their legs and drown them, or was it something else—but then it fell away.

In only her underwear, Hailey felt the elation of lightness and freedom from that dress that had felt as if it was trying, constantly, to drag her down beneath the water. But then she became aware of how she was clinging to her rescuer, her every nerve singing.

With a sense of danger or elation?

Neither. It was surely a sense of being alive.

She was alive and it made her awareness of everything—the sky, the water and especially him—throb through her veins.

Primal.

But then her mind kicked back in. Rational. Wary.

Telling her that just because the danger of the sea had been tamed for now did not mean that there were not other dangers.

Like one of those video games: just when you thought you were safe, up popped another monster.

Not that the man in front of her looked like a monster. The antithesis of one, in fact. And yet, there it was.

The warning light in the distance. Blinking insistently.

Danger. Danger. Danger.

CHAPTER THREE

HER RESCUER LOOKED at Hailey quizzically, as if she had said the word *danger* out loud. But then his attention diverted to the other swimmer in the water, who was speaking.

"I called for the Jet Ski," the other man said. "They'll attach the rescue sled."

"You brought your cell phone?" her rescuer asked, astonished.

"Waterproof."

"What about the Jet Ski running us over?"

"I gave them GPS coordinates."

"Huh," her rescuer said, "you'd almost think you'd done this for a living."

Almost instantly, she could hear the high-pitched whine of engines piercing the quiet of the night, a quiet that had been, just moments ago, a suffocating reminder of how alone she had been. The noise made the throbbing danger sign in her head blink less brilliantly, and she allowed the relief to flow back in along the edges of her distress.

For the first time, tears came: relief, exhaustion, confusion.

"We're almost there," he told her, his voice calm, but his male discomfort with tears palpable. He tried to distract her.

"What's your name?" he asked, conversationally, as if they were both sitting at a bar and he'd offered to buy her a drink.

She felt as if she had to think about it. Finally, her name appeared like in a bubble, in her mind.

"Hailey," she said. Saying her name had a strangeness to it, as if she'd stumbled on a correct answer during a quiz.

"Hailey," he repeated, and her name on his tongue sounded like a benediction. "I'm Gage."

"Gage," she said, "Like on a car? For fuel?"

He cocked his head at her, and a smile tickled across his lips. Was he smiling because he had succeeded at stopping her tears, or because she had made a small joke?

Either way, the upward curve of his lips revealed those straight, white, perfect movie-star teeth that Americans were so famous for.

"Like fuel," he agreed. "Last name is Payton."

Why was he looking at her with sudden intensity, as if he expected a reaction? Oh, wait, the proper reaction would be offering her own last name, wouldn't it?

She went to tell him, but nothing happened. The place where she should have encountered her own surname was mysteriously blank.

"Your first name is a homophone," she said.

Where had that come from? Some fresh panic rose within her. "I don't know my last name."

The other man had been listening, and now he swam closer.

"That's okay," he said soothingly. "I think you're probably in shock. I'm Seth."

He didn't offer his last name, but turned on the flashlight on his beautiful, waterproof phone and waved it in the direction the jet-ski engine noises were coming from.

"They're almost here," he said.

"You'll be warm and dry in no time," Gage assured her.

Her mind felt slow and irrational, and another word tried to edge out the danger sign, which was fading and blinking with less and less intensity.

Safe.

She was going to be safe, soon. Warm. Dry. Had more beautiful words ever been spoken?

"Where did you come from?" she asked, her voice a croak. "How did you hear me? How did you find me? You saved my life."

"Don't tell him that," Seth said with a groan, inserting just the right teasing note of levity into the grave situation. "He'll get bigheaded about it."

She looked into the beautiful perfection of Gage's features, the flawlessness of his skin, and took in his bone structure, the sleek sculpted muscles. She saw the easy assurance in him, the absolute confidence, and the danger sign winked back on. If ever a man had a right to be bigheaded it was probably him.

The kind of man who led a charmed life. Who could call women to him like flowers called bees, like magnets attract steel, like the waves were called to the shore.

Who could hurt a woman. Very badly.

But where had that thought come from? It washed her in guilt. How could she possibly know such a thing when she didn't even know her own last name?

Shouldn't she be feeling only gratitude toward Gage and Seth? It made her feel a bit ashamed that, though she didn't even know her last name, some part of her was in good shape. And that part was wary. Maybe even jaundiced.

Bitter?

The truth was she found him exceedingly attractive. And she realized it wasn't him, precisely, making her awareness of danger so acute.

It was the *attraction* that felt dangerous, that felt like it must be fought at all costs, no matter how vulnerable and grateful she felt.

Her tired mind vowed, for her own protection, that Gage must never know how he was making her long for something that somehow she remembered she could not have.

"What I'd like to know," Gage said, "is where you came from?"

Hailey cast about in her mind. All that was there

was that acute awareness that there were things she could not have.

All else was behind a wall of a terrifying blankness. “I—I—I don't know.”

“Do you think you lost consciousness?”

She contemplated that. “Maybe. Because I don't know how I got in the water. I just remember I was wet and coughing up water, and it was dark, and the current was pulling me away from shore.And that damned dress was pulling at me.”

“So you swallowed water?”

“Yes, definitely.”

The two men exchanged glances.

“Secondary drowning a possibility?” Gage said in an undertone to the other.

A lifted shoulder, *yes*.

“Are you hurt?” Gage asked. “Any pain?”

She thought about that. Between exhilaration, relief, exhaustion, sensation, confusion, she hadn't noticed anything else. But now she took a quick inventory. “My head hurts.”

“Okay. We're going to get you looked after.”

“How did you find yourself in this pickle, darling?” Gage asked.

“Pickle?” she asked, baffled. Her mind went *pickle*, *pickle*, *pickle*, casting around for what that meant, what that was.

“Shock,” Seth said again. “Possible confusion due to head injury.” Then to Gage, “A topic you know quite a bit about.”

The Jet Skis drawing closer drowned out further

conversation. And then, they were there, bathing the three people in the water in the white light of their lamps.

A sea that had just minutes ago seemed endlessly empty was buzzing with light and noise and activity as engines were cut and more people entered the water.

"Miss," a stranger's voice said. "I'll help you onto the sled."

She was embarrassed to find she couldn't let go of Gage.

It's okay," he told the other man. "I've got her." And then he looked at her.

"I've got you, Polo," he told her firmly, "and I'm not letting you go."

Then the man who had saved her life maneuvered Hailey to the side of a tiny life raft that bobbed behind one of the Jet Skis.

"Okay," he told her, "up we go."

Strong hands encircled her waist and she was heaved up onto the rescue sled. She was out of the water, the night air playing across her pebbled flesh.

A strange mixture of exhaustion, euphoria and guardedness filled her, as Gage followed her onto it. His weight, joining hers, rocked the tiny vessel. Not wanting to get dumped back into the sea, she clutched onto him, the rock-hardness of his bicep muscle beneath her fingertips jolting her with more awareness of him. She made herself let go, even as she recognized the weakness of not wanting to.

The craft was probably only made to accommodate one person, so they were squished together. Just as it pierced her awareness that she was only in her underwear and it was probably nearly transparent, a blanket was tossed to them from one of the bobbing skis.

Gage caught it, unfolded it and tucked it tight around her. She closed her eyes against the pull of what she perceived as a certain tender protectiveness. Even through the thin barrier of the blanket, she could feel the contact between them, the hard length of his muscled body, the heat that pumped off him like a furnace.

Keeping her guard up suddenly seemed silly, as if it just took too much effort. She relished the snug sense of warmth and safety, which was such a mind-blowing contrast to her desperation in the water only minutes ago. Her awareness that life could change in a hair was sharp and intoxicating.

The whine of the Jet Ski was deafening, so there was no conversation between them, but words would have felt tiny and insubstantial after what they had just been through. They were whisked along, droplets of water raining down on them, as the stars winked in the night sky above them.

Light began to splash over them and then intensified. Suddenly, they were in a pool of brilliance, chatter rising all around them, as the Jet Ski maneuvered the rescue sled into place. Hailey assumed they were at a dock.

Land.

She could not wait to be completely out of the jaws of the sea and have her feet planted on solid ground!

There was a sense of needing to get away from the man who had rescued her, a feeling that if she stayed around him much longer she would never be able to give him up, like an addict chasing euphoria. He had rescued her, and it was easy to see how you could get an incurable case of hero worship, want to keep this bond forever.

That was a layer of complication she felt unable to deal with.

Gage made her feel grateful, of course. Aware of him—naturally! But also deeply wary and vulnerable. She was tired, she was distressed, she was relieved. This chaotic state of mind could make her do or say regrettable, foolish, totally out-of-character things.

Not that she was totally certain what her character was, but she was pretty sure it was not that of a woman who did and said the kind of things that men like him probably were exposed to quite a lot!

CHAPTER FOUR

GAGE TUCKED THE blanket completely and tightly around Hailey. Then, he found her hand through one of the folds and helped her to her feet. The sled wobbled dangerously beneath her, but hands reached for her from the dock, as Gage lifted her toward them.

He let go of her for the first time since he had swum up to her, and she immediately felt the loss of his touch. This was why it was so important to say goodbye to him as quickly as possible. Because after less than an hour in his company, she felt like a puppy being taken from its litter.

She looked around, trying to get her bearings. Because she knew Seth had used his cell phone and called it in, she was expecting blue and red flashing lights, an ambulance, at the very least. Maybe police. A crowd of helpful people. Fishing boats bobbing quietly at their moorings.

Possibly a brass band, her exhausted mind teased her.

Slowly, and with some shock, Hailey came to realize she was not on a dock at all. There were no fishing boats, no ambulance and certainly no brass band. They had not made landfall.

In fact, Hailey was on the back lower deck of a boat. It was obviously the entry point to the vessel, but also, from the Styrofoam noodles, inflatable toys, stand-up boards and paddles, stored neatly on hooks on the walls, a staging area for water activities.

Even though it was not what she expected—one more thing for her tired mind to grapple with—the water toys in the area assured her as much as the hands reaching out to help her that she had left the cold dark place of certain death behind her.

She bit her lip to keep from bursting into tears again, and looked around, trying to make sense of her landing place.

It was apparent to her that this was nothing like any boat she had ever seen before. Her eyes moved to stainless steel railings that led up curving symmetrical staircases on either side of a door at the rear and center of the platform. She tilted her head and looked up. A name written in gold cursive shone in the abundance of light.

Seas du Jour.

She tilted her head back farther and saw the sleek, soaring lines of the back of the boat, brilliant white walls, stainless-steel-railed decks and steel-framed windows and portholes. Everything sparkled, astonishingly clean as if it had been freshly polished. The word *boat*, of course, did not do the vessel justice.

Somehow, though she had certainly never been on one, she knew this was a yacht. But that word didn't seem to do it justice, either.

The vessel was like a floating castle, a dazzling enchantment.

For a moment, her poor mind wondered if any of it was real. Maybe she had died out there in the water.

Maybe this was heaven.

And maybe Gage Payton, in all his perfection, was not a man at all, but an angel.

Gage's voice separated from the other voices around Hailey. "Take her to the VIP suite. Send for a doctor, right away."

Definitely a man, not an angel. Definitely a boat—an extraordinarily posh one to be sure—but not heaven.

She blearily contemplated the authority in his voice, heard Seth respond that a doctor was already on his way. She felt as if she should really insist that they take her to shore and to a doctor—not bring a doctor to her. She really felt as if she should insist she was in charge of her own life.

Grateful for the rescue, but nonetheless, she would take it from here!

But Hailey realized the effort of being in charge of her own life was going to have to wait, because right now it seemed like a mountain she could not climb.

Then, just like that, she was surrounded by several men dressed in crisp white T-shirts and pressed navy blue shorts. A wheelchair appeared from somewhere.

"Oh, I don't need that," Hailey protested.

It was one final effort to grab back some control, but suddenly she found her legs in danger of collapsing out from under her, and she wound up sinking into the chair.

Embarrassed, she wondered if she was going to be carried in that wheelchair up one of those two curving staircases, like a queen on a palanquin.

But, no, she was turned, and faced the door at the center of the platform. One of the crew rushed to open it and her mouth dropped. Because behind that door was an elevator.

She was shepherded in by two crew members and wheeled around, facing front again. Even with the three of them in here, the elevator did not feel cramped. She was turned just in time to see Seth tossing a towel to Gage, who was still facing the sea.

She could see he was even taller than she had imagined. Water ran in silvery rivulets off the curls of his hair and down the broadness of his naked back. He was wearing swimming shorts—board shorts, she thought they were called—but the normally loose-fitting apparel was so soaked they clung to every perfect line of him.

As dazed as she was, thanks to Gage, Hailey was not dead. A woman would have to be dead not to notice he was beautifully made. Bathed in the lights from the deck, he looked as perfect as a marble statue, David breathed to life by Michelangelo's vision.

A reluctant sense of *aliveness* further challenged her desire to take control of something—anything—but no, she could not drag her eyes away from him. She was startlingly aware of Gage's incredible golden skin tone, his hair curling around his neck, the sweep of broad shoulders, his wide back narrowing to his hips. He had the sweetest little dimples on either side of the base of his spine, where it dipped into the sodden shorts. She shamelessly admired the muscular cut of his buttocks beneath the thin, wet fabric that looked as if they had been chiseled out of stone by that master artist.

As if he sensed someone watching, Gage glanced over his shoulder and caught her staring. He turned slightly, tilted his head at her with such masculine self-assuredness she felt herself recoil. The small smile that tickled the lush fullness of his lips, that revealed the flawless line of his white teeth, made the coil of trepidation curl tighter in her stomach.

What was it about his unabashed certainty in his own masculinity that made her feel as if she either wanted to run away or cast herself upon him and kiss him until they were both breathless?

Thankfully, the elevator doors whispered shut.

As the elevator ascended out of its port, she saw it was completely glass-encased, encircled by what appeared to be stainless steel bands. It looked and felt like an ornate birdcage. And she was the bird caught in it! She could momentarily see the deck again, Gage bare-chested, still dripping water and bathed in moonlight.

She looked away quickly and took in the stunning views: a lighthouse and a village in the distance. Too many things were fighting for the attention of her beleaguered mind now. She turned it to the posh interior of the elevator cage. There was a control panel of buttons subtly labeled with the decks.

The elevator came to a smooth halt and the doors whooshed quietly open. She could not prevent a gasp of utter astonishment as she was wheeled off. She had been in hotels that were not this luxurious!

But as soon as she thought that, she could feel that alarming sense of fogginess. What hotels? Where?

She was ushered through a gorgeous lounge with deep leather chairs, a bar, pool table and huge television set that had dropped from the ceiling. The opulence of that room should have prepared her for the VIP stateroom, but it didn't.

Hailey looked around, reluctantly entranced, as she was pushed through the double doors into the suite. The luxury was evident everywhere. Two deep club chairs faced a fireplace. A fireplace on a boat seemed as inconceivable as the elevator had been.

There was a TV set above it. A bed was on the other wall—round, pillowed, the linens luxurious and neutral. The walls displayed gorgeous art pieces, relief sculptures in metal and wood, as well as amazing abstract paintings. Thick floor-to-ceiling draperies were pulled closed over what appeared to be an entire wall of windows.

She was aware shock was setting in, her system trying to cope with a sense of too much, from near death in the sea to this: finding herself a guest on a luxury yacht such as most people couldn't even imagine. It had three stories! And an elevator. A fireplace. Priceless art. And she had only seen a fraction of it so far.

The funniest thing was that all this stunning buffet for the senses paled in comparison to the rather startling moment of seeing Gage standing on the deck with water sluicing off his naked chest.

"Ma'am? I'm Troy. And this is Jason."

"Hailey," she said, grateful he had not given last names.

"I'm the medic on this vessel," Troy said. Like Seth and Gage, his accent was American.

He held up his fingers for her. "How many do you see?"

"Three."

"Excellent," he said, and she felt a little pleased with herself.

"Year?"

That one seemed harder. She made herself answer with confidence even though she wasn't quite sure.

"Excellent," he said again, and she felt relieved. But after that, she didn't get any more questions right. She didn't know the day of the week, and she certainly didn't know who the president of the United States was.

Still, he seemed unperturbed. "Can I help you get in the bed? The doctor is on his way."

She slid a look at the bed and felt a pull of pure wanting that she felt it was imperative to fight.

"I'll just stay in the wheelchair until he gets here," she said. Giving in to the temptation of the bed could erase whatever was left of her ability to be in control of her own destiny.

"I'm not sure how long he'll be. I'd like to do a preliminary examination, and it would be easier for me if you were on the bed."

She squinted at him suspiciously. Was he just saying that to make her feel as if she was helping him and not the other way around?

"It'll be warmer," he said persuasively, "and way more comfortable."

She looked at the bed and could imagine herself sinking into it.

"At the very least, you have to get out of those wet things. I brought you a T-shirt to slip on. I can ask one of the female staff to come and help you, if you like?"

There was that alarmed feeling again.

"I don't need anyone's help," she said and snatched the T-shirt from him. She tried to soften her reaction. "But thank you."

The two men left the room, and she got out of the wheelchair. Her legs felt like rubber and she was shaking. She dropped the blanket and struggled out of her wet underthings. Finally, they fell away from her, and she slipped the T-shirt on.

It was brilliant white and way too large, coming down to her knees, but still, it felt wonderfully clean and dry.

She eyed the bed, sighed and moved over to it. What was she afraid would happen if she gave in?

She slid between crisp sheets, as brilliantly white as the T-shirt. The bed was so extravagantly soft it felt as if she had lain down on a cloud. This was what she had feared: giving in made her want to surrender, let someone else be in control.

It was without a doubt the biggest, most comfortable bed she had ever been in.

But was it? Suddenly, she felt unsure. She tried to picture a bed—any bed, her bed at home, her childhood bed—but that place in her mind was a startling blank. Even *home* seemed like only a word. There was no image attached to it.

Troy, all efficiency and professionalism, came back in, and Jason stood quietly just inside the door.

She appreciated the propriety of it. Troy took her pulse and her temperature, then used a stethoscope to listen to her chest. He gently manipulated each of her limbs, asking about pain.

It was only when he touched the back of her head that she winced.

"That hurts?"

"Something awful," she said and then reached back and touched where the pain was radiating from. More shocking than her hand coming away covered in blood was the fact her hair was apparently short. Very short.

She was baffled. Didn't she have long hair?

"A bit of a scrape there," Troy said, calmly concluding, perhaps, that the sudden confusion on her face was because of the blood and not the short bristles of hair she had just encountered.

He took her hand and wiped the blood off it. Hailey was fairly certain he was minimizing whatever he saw. "Head wounds can bleed quite a bit."

She felt a surge of panic. Why was her head bleeding? Why was her hair short? And where on earth was she?

The panic settled slightly when the door opened and Gage came in. She locked in on him.

Despite a multitude of mixed-up feelings rising in her every time she saw him, he felt like her touchstone. He had changed out of his soaked shorts and was now wearing casual pants, tan-colored and pressed, and a navy blue T-shirt with an American football embossed over one breast.

He had incredibly long, muscled legs, and the shirt molded the lines and mounds of the chest she had come to know so intimately out there in the dark water.

She felt compelled to drink in his skin, which was a shade of gold as inviting as a loaf of bread just removed from the oven. The gorgeous tangle of his damp curls came almost to his shoulders. In the subdued light of the bedroom, she could see his hair, dry, would be the exact shade of melted dark chocolate.

His nose had a strong line and his cheekbones were high-cut. He was bearded, which drew attention to his full, wide lips, and did not hide the fact his chin had the tiniest little dent in it—not quite a cleft, more like a dimple.

But it was his eyes that were absolutely mesmerizing: almond-shaped, framed in an abundance of long lashes, a color like moss-covered stone, green with gray beneath it, sparkling with strength and resolve and a touch of humor.

He made her feel like he would be a very good choice if she was going to give up control to someone. But then that made her feel weak and she sensed that right now, especially, she needed to dig deep, to find whatever was left inside her that could be strong.

"Relax. You're safe. Everything is going to be okay."

As tempting as it was to believe him, Hailey could feel confusion rising up in her.

"That's easy for you to say, but I don't who I am, I don't know where I am, and I certainly don't know how I ended up in the ocean," she told him. Plus, she didn't know where her hair was. Just articulating parts of her predicament made her feel as if she was going to start hyperventilating.

"Take a deep breath," he said quietly, reading her growing agitation with accuracy. "Through your nose. Pretend you're smelling a flower. Perfect.

Now blow it out through your mouth, like you're blowing out a candle."

Reluctantly, she did as he asked. More loss of control. Now, she was even being instructed how to breathe!

All the more annoying, it worked. She could feel her agitation reducing ever so slightly.

"You're going to be okay, Hailey."

She felt unexpectedly calmed by his voice and his presence, and especially, strangely, by his use of her name. She allowed herself to follow his instruction, as if it was an order.

Relax. Breathe in. Blow out. She sank back against the pillows and allowed the comfort of the steady rhythm to lull her. The bed was rocking gently with the motion of the sea moving beneath the boat. She imagined maybe this was what it felt like to be in a cradle. She could feel her eyes closing…

CHAPTER FIVE

GAGE TOUCHED HER SHOULDER. "Sorry. No going to sleep."

Hailey desperately wanted to. She'd known accepting the invitation of the bed had been a mistake.

"You have to stay with us for a while longer," Gage said. His voice was quiet but firm. "Until the doctor has had a look at you."

"Yes, about the doctor," she said. "Don't you think I should be going to hospital?" Her head hurt really badly. But she was so tired. Now the thought of getting back out of the bed was more than she could bear. Even if she wasn't allowed to sleep, it felt good to be here.

"The doctor will come soon. He'll decide what the next steps are." Gage cocked his head. "In fact, I think he's arriving now."

She listened, too. The sound grew steadily louder, distinctive.

Whop-whop-whop.

She wondered exactly where she was that the doctor had to come by helicopter.

* * *

The doctor had come and gone. He had found no indication of drug or alcohol impairment in the patient, so that could be ruled out as the reason she had ended up in the ocean. Gage had a list of instructions—as if he needed those, world expert on concussion that he was—and information.

No secondary drowning, thank goodness—her lungs were clear. But she definitely had temporary amnesia, a result of a head wound of unknown origin, possibly complicated by trauma.

The doctor told him he had given Hailey as much medication as her injuries allowed. The doc thought, since she was settled and comfortable here, and the ship had their own medical staff, that it would be better if she stayed the night. In the morning, he would arrange for her to be moved.

Gage opened the door and peeked back in the room, hoping Hailey would be sleeping.

She was sitting up, her head wound tight with bandages. She looked tiny and fragile in the large bed. Her skin was nearly as white as the sheets. Her eyes, blue as a summer sky in Iowa, were wide and huge, though he detected something slightly dazed in her expression.

Troy gave Gage a look—a warning of some sort?—and then left the room.

"I'm not the star of a mummy movie," Hailey told Gage. She narrowed her eyes at him and looked faintly combative.

He crossed the room, stood beside the bed and regarded her.

"You're not?" he teased, gently. "Are you sure? Because I'm pretty certain I saw you in *Curse of the Mummy*. The little feisty one that you really had to watch out for."

Gage watched Hailey mull over his suggestion.

Finally, she said, "Did the little feisty one look awful?"

He cocked his head at her. "Well, kind of cute actually, as much as a mummy can be."

He realized he did think she was very cute, and it seemed weirdly inappropriate, as if he was the doctor and a certain professional distance had to be maintained.

Thankfully, she did not fixate on the topic of cuteness.

"At least my hair is hidden," she said and then fixed him with a faintly accusing look. "Do you know what happened to it?"

"Something happened to your hair?" Little bits of it were sticking out on the crown of her head where the bandage was not wrapped. They looked a bit like porcupine quills.

"It's supposed to be long."

"Oh," he said, a little confused.

Her words were definitely slurred. When he looked more closely, her eyes seemed to be going in different directions. Maybe more, then, than slightly dazed. Unless Gage was mistaken—and he was pretty sure he was not—this is what Troy had tried to convey to him. Hailey, as a result of those doctor-administered medications, was stoned out of her gourd.

"The doctor said it's okay if you go to sleep now. But I should warn you—someone has to wake you up every hour or so and shine a light in your eyes to check for dilation. If you feel sick or your headache gets worse, there'll be somebody here with you. Let them know right away."

"Did you know you sound like a cowboy?" she asked, as if she hadn't heard a word he'd said.

"I didn't," he humored her. "I'm from Iowa, not exactly cowboy country. I'm not sure what you think a cowboy sounds like."

She drawled the word *darlin'*. "Like that. So you aren't one?"

"Not even close."

"Maybe all American men sound like cowboys," she decided.

He thought of his cousin from Boston. Nope.

"Do you like cowboys?" she asked.

"If they have Dallas in front of that name, yes."

She didn't get that reference, at all, which probably meant she knew nothing about American football. Why feel so relieved? The doctor had said he would make arrangements to get her ashore first thing in the morning.

"A cowboy would be the American equivalent of a knight," she explained to him patiently. "Saving the maiden in distress."

"Oh," he said uneasily.

She gave a little hiccuping giggle. "Me."

"Okay," he said slowly. "Thank you for clarifying that. I'm not any kind of hero, if that's what you're thinking."

Little lady, don't pin your hopes on me.

"I wasn't thinking that!" she said, way too quickly. "Though you did save me. I'm very grateful. Don't think I'm not. But I have to get away from you."

She said this with quite a bit of vehemence.

"Oh?" he said. It stunned him just a tiny bit, because in his experience most women did not want to get away from him.

The exact opposite in fact. But what kind of women? His sister, always frank, had frequently teased him about what she called his Bouncy Brigade and claimed that in order to date her brother a woman only had to qualify with three B's: built, blonde, brainless.

Naturally, her criticism—no matter how lightly couched—had made him pretend he would rather die than live her wholesome small-town life, which had been his parents' life, too. In actual fact, he was aware of a secret longing for something similar that he could not afford to focus on. Why give energy to what you could never have? Even before the incident with Babba he had seen that a normal life was becoming a place in the far distance that he had less and less hope of returning to. Gage had now started to dedicate his considerable energy and passion to building his business instead.

Hailey moved on. She sighed, heavily. "The doctor said I have..."

"To go to sleep?" he suggested.

She closed her eyes, as if she was obeying, and he just thought she had drifted off, when her eyes popped back open.

"Anesthesia!" she crowed. "The doctor says I have anesthesia."

"Amnesia," he corrected her mildly.

She waved a hand dismissively. "He said my memory will come back in an hour."

Gage had also talked to the doctor. What the man had said was that her memory would probably come back within twenty-four to forty-eight hours. She had suffered a bad blow to her head, but no fracture. Her current state was probably being compounded by shock and possibly trauma.

"I thought he'd never stop asking questions. Worse than Troy's questions," she said, "Honestly? I thought he'd never shut up."

And then in a slurred voice, Hailey made a little song out of the doctor's questions. He thought he could vaguely pick out the sea shanty tune of "Drunken Sailor."

What day is it, it?
Where are you from, from?
Where are you staying, staying?
How did you get in the water, water?

Gage felt his lips twitching as she obviously felt saying the word twice at the end of every sentence added a bit of cadence.

How long were you in the water, water?
What's your last name, name?
Are you somebody's wife, wife?
Are you traveling with a friend, friend?
Do you think anyone is looking for you, you?
Who should we notify that you've been found, found?

Well, one thing he knew about her for sure: she had no musical talent, either as a composer or a singer.

"You know how many questions I got right?" she demanded.

He shook his head.

She put her index finger and thumb together and waved a zero in front of him.

"I'm sorry," he said.

"I hate failing tests," she told him, mournfully. "I'm really very smart. At least I think I am. I'm not really sure though. Because of the Anastasia."

"I'm sure you're very smart," he said, mollifying her. "Because probably only a dozen or so people in the whole world know what a homophone is."

"Your name," she said.

"A word that sounds the same but is spelled differently and has different meanings. For example g-a-g-e and g-a-u-g-e. And don't mistake me for smart. I had to look it up."

"Did the doctor cut my hair?" she suddenly asked.

He thought of that otter-slick hair in the water. He shook his head.

"Hmm," she said, "maybe it was for the movie."

"What movie?"

"I think I might be in a movie. I don't think it's about mummies, even if I do look like the cute one you have to watch out for," she decided. "Spy thriller. I'm in a double-oh-seven movie. Look around. Movie set, right?"

"I guess," he said, trying, again, to suppress laughter.

"Doctor arrives by helicopter," she told him sagely, as if she had detected he might need convincing. "He probably got lowered onto the boat by a rope."

"There's actually a helicopter landing pad."

She took that in, nodded slowly and gazed off into the distance.

"Exactly," she said finally. "A helicopter landing pad on a boat. Is this called a boat? Is it still a boat if you can land a helicopter on it? Or is it like a megayacht? I saw one once on television."

"Oh," he said, "I think, technically, any vessel that floats is a boat."

She began humming what he recognized as the theme music for a different spy movie franchise to the one she'd just mentioned.

"Double-oh-seven," she said sternly, and Gage

realized she was speaking to him. "Unless you prefer Agent Marco?"

"We can go with double-oh."

"Good! Your mission, should you choose to accept it, is to find out about the pillows."

"The pillows?"

"I bled on the pillows," she whispered. "I fear they're now ruined."

"Don't worry about the pillows," he said.

She was undeterred.

"But I think they're very valuable," Hailey confided in him. Despite just surviving a near catastrophe—her voice was still raspy from swallowing sea water—her tiny bow of a mouth flattened into a stubborn downturn, as if she needed to make this point urgently.

"It's not worth worrying about. Really."

She considered that, not pleased, either that he was not getting the importance of the pillows, or that he was making the decision about what she should worry about.

"Unless the pillows belong to you, that seems a bit presumptuous," she said, sounding out each syllable of *presumptuous* with great care. She leveled a stern look at him. It might have been very stern indeed, if she had been able to keep her eyes from sliding in two different directions.

Now did not seem like the best time to reveal that the yacht and everything in it—including the damn pillows—did belong to him.

"Presumptuous," Gage said, deciding for a teasing note in light of her injuries. "You seem very—"

He was going to say British, but she cut him off.

"Persnickety? Perhaps I'll take that as my agent name. Agent Persnickety. On the other hand, I might prefer to be a mummy."

She fingered the sheets. "I think they could be Egyptian cotton." She snapped her fingers. Well, attempted to snap. The result was more like the muffled sound of the top of a pen being clicked.

"Am I in Egypt?" she asked.

It hadn't even occurred to him that she didn't know what country she was in. He didn't let his concern for the way her thoughts were jumping around show on his face. "No."

"America, then? Everyone, including you, has cowboy accents. Except the doctor didn't. I wonder where he was from?"

"He was Greek. You're in Greece."

"Greece?" she repeated, astounded. "Like in *Mamma Mia*?"

"Sorry?"

"A movie," she said. "Or a musical. Live theater. I adore live theater."

"There? See? Your memory is coming back to you already."

"You're right. It is. I remember the song."

She attempted to snap again with her fingers. And failed again. Then she sang a snippet of a song, presumably from that musical movie, about knowing better and still finding someone irresistible.

She stopped her serenade suddenly, studied him carefully. She seemed to be looking at his lips.

"You know what I don't remember?" she announced in a whisper. "If I've ever kissed a man with facial hair. I think I'd remember doing that, don't you?"

"Ah, I don't know."

The awkwardness of his answer seemed to alert her that maybe the question was a bit off, because she blushed. Deeply.

And then said, in a rush, "The doctor said he'll arrange for me to go to hospital. I don't know when though. Soon, I hope."

"He's going to call me when it's arranged."

"That's good," she said. Gage looked at her. And then to his great relief, her eyes clicked closed, like one of those dolls his niece had.

It wasn't until a little whisper of breath came out of her slightly pursed lips that he realized he'd been holding his.

It was probably wrong to be so happy she had conked out.

How did a guy take an announcement that she didn't remember if she'd been kissed by a man with a beard? As an invitation?

Yeah. To run.

Still, Gage could not resist looking at her a little longer. A shiver went along his spine when he realized how very close she had come to dying.

He had thought her hair was dark, but now it was drying, that little tuft sticking out of the bandages was a rich honey-colored shade of light brown, a tint or two darker than blond.

She wasn't beautiful, and he would know—for the past decade he'd been surrounded by some of the world's most beautiful and sophisticated women.

No, the woman before him, with her little smattering of freckles and her every-which-way drying hair poking out from under bandages, her bow of a mouth and those huge sea-blue eyes was cute without even trying.

She didn't have on a scrap of makeup. He supposed it might have washed off in the ocean, though in his understanding makeup usually left some pretty ugly hints if it was dissolved by salt water, either tears or the sea.

His experience, admittedly, was more with tears, which he had seen plenty of when he'd been unwilling to step up to the role of being anyone's knight. Or cowboy, as the case may be.

And he had to keep that foremost in his mind as he wondered about the most natural question.

Was the kiss comment just an observation on her memory loss? Kind of like saying, *I don't think I've ever been to Paris*, or *I don't think I've ever ridden a horse*? Or did it mean she *wanted* to be kissed by a man with facial hair?

CHAPTER SIX

WHEN HE'D FIRST been drafted to the NFL, Gage had been with the same girl, Molly, who he'd dated all through college. She'd, predictably, been on the cheerleading squad, always keeping her grades right on the cusp of getting kicked off the squad and maybe out of school.

His draft had required a move to a new city, and she came with him. One year behind him, she'd made the choice not to finish her degree. They hadn't really discussed it. He'd been twenty-three. What do twenty-three-year-olds *discuss*?

He'd moved. His girlfriend had moved with him. That had seemed solid in a world in which he was bombarded with changes.

What he hadn't been prepared for was how *his* fame had caused a stunning metamorphosis in *her*.

Her auburn hair was suddenly bleached blond. She wore false eyelashes. She had something injected in her lips. The huge closet in the too-large apartment they'd rented was stuffed with designer bags and more clothing and shoes than it seemed like one person could possibly wear in a lifetime.

Molly courted the attention of the celebrities who now sought him out. She wanted to party. She loved not having to wait in lines at nightclubs. She loved the red carpet. The constant invitations opened doors to a world that she had only seen on television before.

What he wanted was to succeed at football, period—something that required hard work, discipline and single-minded focus.

Not parties being brought home to his apartment at three in the morning.

Not fights about credit card bills and extravagant shoes.

Despite the fact they were not getting along, Molly started pushing to get married. He resisted. She pushed even harder.

Then Molly had left out the brochure for a plastic surgeon. She'd wanted breast augmentation.

He'd been stunned.

There was absolutely nothing wrong with the way she was made. He'd told her he hoped he had never made her feel that way.

And that's when he'd found out it wasn't about him, at all.

It was in that moment that he realized this—or possibly *Molly*—was not in his game plan. He'd been honest with her, and as gentle as a twenty-something career athlete was capable of being, which was probably not very.

Still, he didn't think he'd deserved the absolute shellacking he'd gotten from the press and social media, most of it fueled by Molly airing her every grievance—complaints that he, insensitive cretin that he was—a direct quote—had been unaware of and some of which were totally fabricated.

He didn't think people should know if he squeezed the toothpaste in the middle and left the seat up. He didn't think they should care.

But, oh, how they did.

After that, he'd always been crystal clear with anyone he'd dated about his relationship game plan. While he was still active in his career, he told them, it was his obsession and his passion and it came first; he did not see himself settling down.

After being so clear, he'd been taken aback when whoever he was dating thought she could change his mind as easy as you could change a game plan during the first quarter.

They'd known before he had, apparently, that he was "Catch of the Century."

After his career had come to an abrupt end, he had briefly considered revisiting his game plan, had allowed himself to think *maybe* he could have a family life, that soft place to fall, that one place in all the world where it was safe to be yourself.

In other words, he had found himself longing for a place—or maybe it was a feeling—of home.

But after Babba's betrayal? How did you ever overcome the fear that if you let people get too close to you, they would only hurt you? When you were as well-known as he was, what were the chances of him ever being loved for himself and not his money?

No, much better to take up with the Bouncy Brigade, a string of superficial relationships that in the end had left him feeling more exhausted, disillusioned and empty than he'd felt without them.

Which explained why he had then given up dating, entirely. No one could be trusted.

No one. It was too much effort, and failure was so painful, it was not even worth trying.

He looked at Hailey's fingers, where they were clutching the top of the sheet, not looking very relaxed, despite the fact she was out like a light.

No nail polish. No professional manicure. Tidy nails.

No rings.

A ring would be nice, and good protection.

Against what? he asked himself, annoyed.

The little feisty one that you really had to watch out for.

Troy was waiting in the hallway right outside the door.

"What did the doc give her?" Gage asked him dryly. "A horse tranquilizer?"

"I think she just had that over-the-top reaction because she's so small. She's dehydrated, too, not to mention exhausted. I'll make sure she drinks something every time I wake her up to check on her."

"Good, thanks."

Gage went in search of the man he could always

count on for some sober advice. And who was really good at game plans.

Gage tried to put Hailey out of his mind, but no, she was stuck there, his own customary discipline shredded, as the dramatic events of the evening caught up with him.

The truth was she seemed adorable, like a wet kitten who had been rescued from a rain barrel. Despite her accent placing her a world away from where he had grown up, her concern for the pillows reminded him of his own middle-class upbringing where people were careful with the things they had worked so hard for.

She had seemed wholesome and without guile; even her comment about the kiss had seemed more out of curiosity than passion.

He wasn't sure how he could know that, based on the events that had recently happened to them, though of course that kind of shared experience could lead you to a sense—probably a false one—of knowing someone.

Hailey didn't even know herself yet, he reminded himself grimly.

Molly had never been what he would call wholesome. A popular girl, yes, and really fun. It wasn't until later he'd realized she was inordinately interested in herself, her appearance, her possessions, her calendar—and social media.

Now, she was a double D, and gracing the pages of the tabloids in her tight leather pants because she was dating an aging rock star. She was still, years after their split, referred to as Gage Payton's ex.

One thing about Molly—he couldn't imagine her using a word like persnickety or knowing what a homophone was.

In fact, he was not sure he had ever heard anyone use the words *homophone* or *persnickety* before. Maybe not *presumptuous*, either, now that he thought about it. It made him think of those owl-eyed girls who loved the library and walked home with stacks of books hugged to their chests.

The kind of girls he, unapologetic jock, had never gone for. He was willing to bet Hailey had never been a cheerleader…

He found Seth in his office.

"How is she?" his friend asked.

"Discombobulated." He saw Seth's eyebrows lift, so didn't add *persnickety*. "She's got a pretty significant wound on her head. She's wrapped up like a mummy."

The feisty one that you have to watch out for.

"The doctor says she has temporary amnesia. He gave her something pretty potent for pain relief. She's all over the place. Singing. Talking about movies. Worried about pillows. She doesn't seem to have a clue where she is. Not even what country."

The adrenaline was beginning to drain out of him. That euphoric feeling of having triumphed, of needing to protect her, was being replaced with a tired kind of cynicism.

Now that he wasn't under the influence of those

blue eyes, he felt a returning deep need to guard himself.

"Or so she says." He suddenly felt as if he'd been charmed, and that his customary guard might have been bashed by the rescue.

Seth lifted an eyebrow. "I don't think anyone's that good an actress."

"Say that to someone who hasn't dated actresses."

"You might have a point there."

"I've had a lot of head injuries," Gage pushed on. "So have you. Have you ever completely lost your memory from it?"

Seth shook his head slowly.

"I mean how could she know what Egyptian cotton is, but not know where she is? How could she know things about double-oh-seven and *Mamma Mia* but not know who she is? How could she pull a word like homophone out of her head and not know her last name?"

"It sounds as if a very interesting conversation was had. *Mamma Mia*, huh?"

"If you start singing, I'm firing you."

"Promise or threat?" Seth teased but then became serious. "The mind is a complicated mechanism. I wouldn't rule out anything."

"Still, amnesia? I don't know. You read about it, or see it in movies. But in real life? How common is it?"

Seth looked at him steadily. He knew exactly where Gage was coming from. "You think she was swimming out to the yacht to deliberately engineer an encounter with you?"

Put like that, he knew it sounded ridiculous. On the other hand… "Weirder things have happened," he reminded his friend.

He had been stalked, seriously, three times. He'd had several women he'd never even met claim he was the father of their children. He'd had a woman jump in front of his vehicle. He'd found a naked woman swimming in his pool.

He didn't even pick up his own mail anymore. Seth had hired someone to go through it, assessing threats and making sure crackpots never got past his guard. There was a fan club, somewhere, that looked after everything else, and that he sent signed photos to. Though it was easy to make a signature look real, and that would have made his life easier, he signed them all himself.

A stack of them, once a month, until his hand cramped. Because, for the most part, he appreciated the outpourings of love and support from the majority of his fan base. He'd made a lot of sacrifices to his personal life, but he had also been blessed with abundance beyond measure, and he was aware of that.

Still, for a few, a signed photo—even the real thing—was never going to be enough. That was precisely why Seth was on board. He was on the team to protect him from the shocking lengths that fans—largely female fans—would go to get close to Gage Payton.

It was usually Seth who was overly suspicious, running everything through the filter of possible threats and deceptions.

"Look, I've had a front-row seat for all the craziness you've faced," Seth said now, his tone pensive. "The *Wheeple Magazine* thing brought out the crazies, for sure…but I don't get that feeling this time."

Feelings, Gage thought, were particularly unreliable things and he was surprised it would figure into any kind of threat analysis from Seth.

"Still, I'd rather err on the side of caution," Gage said. "The doctor said they'll arrange for hospitalization tomorrow, and I think that's probably a good solution."

He felt suddenly eager to divest himself of the complication that had arrived so unexpectedly in his life.

Those big eyes, those little tufts of honey-spun hair, the offkey singing…it felt like they could wiggle right by every defense and maybe already had. Just a little bit.

Best to deal with that kind of sneaky, sidewinding threat swiftly.

Seth rocked back in his desk chair, knit his fingers together under his nose and pursed his lips. Gage just knew he wasn't going to like what he had to say.

"So, she doesn't know who she is, she's got no wallet, no ID, no phone. And you're just going to unload her?"

He didn't have to say it like that—as if Gage was the arch villain. In a double-oh-seven movie.

"I'm not going to just abandon her completely. A hospital is probably the best place for her until her memory comes back. Which, according to the doctor, should be fairly quickly."

"Here's the thing. I don't think anyone trying to swim out to the boat to create an encounter with you would have done it in that dress," Seth said.

"We're talking about people with a screw loose," Gage reminded him.

"Well, the women I've seen throwing themselves at you probably would have been more scantily dressed for a swim. And then there's the head injury, which could certainly explain her confusion. You saw blood. That's not been faked."

There was no arguing with that. He remembered her earnest expression as she worried about blood on the pillow.

"You know, she didn't react at all to your name. And I just don't think she was swimming out to find the famous football player with an injury like that on her head."

"You think she slipped on some rocks, hit her head and ended up in the ocean?"

"Possibly. Pulled out by the currents. Or maybe she fell off a boat. Those are certainly two scenarios."

"But?"

"What if somebody did it to her?" Seth's tone

was very soft. "What if someone watched us rescuing her from the water?"

In all that blackness, was it possible a boat had lurked unseen?

"What if they're waiting to finish the job?"

Seth could be trusted to ferret out unwelcome possibilities, but the pure menace of that suggestion curled through Gage like a dark shadow. He sucked in his breath, feeling a shocking and fierce rage at the thought that Hailey ending up in the water might have been the result of an act of violence committed against her.

"I mean, if we gave it to the media," Seth said, "we could probably find out who she was within hours. But I hate to expose her to that kind of attention. Particularly if they find a link to you. You know what they'll be like."

Oh, that he did. They'd feign concern and kindness, but in reality, Hailey would be the story, not a real live person.

They'd take her apart bit by bit and feed the morsels to the sharks if it got them more hits and likes. They would exploit any link to him mercilessly, because he had a known track record for getting the clicks.

"Plus, if someone did do it to her, the publicity could lead them right to her."

"What do you suggest?" Gage asked, tersely.

"I don't feel as if there's a choice. We have to keep her here. I know there's a ninety-nine percent chance she ended up in the water innocently enough. But I think we should err on the side of caution and assume the one percent—that someone did this to her. With that comes the assumption, as remote as it is, that they could still be watching her and waiting for her. Just until we have evidence to the contrary."

Gage nodded, aware his position had just shifted radically from *Must get rid of her* to *Must make her protection a top priority.*

"Let's handle it in-house for forty-eight to seventy-two hours," Seth said.

"Okay."

"I'll get a call in to the police right away to see if there's a missing person's report. And I'll discreetly open up some other channels to start inquiries so that the media doesn't make their latest Gage Payton story about 'girl washed up in Greece with amnesia.'"

"Okay," he said again.

"With any luck," Seth continued, "sooner rather than later, I'll probably know who she is and where she came from. Or maybe she'll have regained some memory by then."

"Fine," Gage agreed.

"We'll need to follow strict concussion protocols. Lucky for us we have one of the world's foremost concussion experts right here."

"Yeah, lucky that," Gage said dryly.

CHAPTER SEVEN

HAILEY WOKE UP and tried to get her bearings.

Her head hurt and she felt unbelievably dry-mouthed and groggy. She had the faintest sensation of self-loathing as if she'd been drinking too much and done something really stupid.

But she hadn't done anything silly like that since college.

College! It felt like a clue she needed to follow, but the effort felt too great and trying to follow the thought seemed to deepen the ache in her head. Instead she allowed herself the slow awareness of the luxurious comfort of the bed, the slight rocking sensation, the feeling of safety.

The room was murky, but bright light was coming through slits on the edges of pulled-down shades. Day had come.

Thoughts crowded around her now, each demanding her attention.

Dark cold water and certain death.

A man—two men—saving her.

Gage, her Marco, had told her last night she was in Greece. What was she doing in Greece? How could she know she did not belong in Greece, but still not have a clue where she did belong?

Where was she from? How had she ended up in the water? What was her last name?

Panic pushed around her feeling of safety like an enemy trying to breach the gates.

And then a scent tickled her nostrils—masculine, ocean-fresh, clean—and the part of her that was panicking went still. She turned her head slightly.

A recliner had been pulled up beside the bed, and Gage was sleeping in it, his feet up, his hands folded across his chest. Throughout the night it had been a man named Troy, hadn't it? She had a memory of him waking her up, several times, asking her a few questions and checking the ability of her pupils to dilate with a small penlight.

When had Gage come in? Still, there he was, the reason for her feeling of safety.

Then another memory came, foggier, the reason for that hangover feeling of self-loathing.

Good grief. She had belted out "Mamma Mia" *to him.*

She touched her head and felt the swathe of bandages. She realized nature called, and she carefully pushed back the covers and tiptoed past Gage to the bathroom. The small effort made her dizzy with effort.

The bathroom—it was called a head on a boat and how did she know that?—was so luxurious it took her breath away.

There were no blackout shades in here, and the

light that poured through the stainless steel-encased porthole was brilliant, even if it caused a smarting sensation behind her eyes. Through the porthole, she could see the deep, deep blue of the endless ocean.

She looked longingly at the jetted tub and the exquisite tiles in the glassed-in shower, but knew she was too wobbly for either.

She had to hold herself up against the sink as she washed her hands and splashed water on her face.

The light that poured in was unforgiving. Hailey took stock. And winced. A too-large T-shirt swam around her. She was pale as a ghost, except for dark circles under her eyes. Even her lips looked pale. Her head was completely encased in bandages, blood seeping around the edges from the back.

A memory of a discussion about mummies made her wince again.

No matter how bad a shock you'd had, you didn't want this particular look while sharing a space with a man who looked like Gage!

She, unfortunately, could not think of any way for improvement. In fact, she touched the little spike of hair that sat on top of her head like a feather on the head of a pony at the circus and wondered if it could be any worse.

She revisited the feeling of disbelief from last night when she'd first discovered she had short hair. That seemed all wrong.

She opened the drawers in the sink cabinet and almost wept with relief when she found neatly stored brand-new toothbrushes, toothpastes and deodorants.

There was one thing she could improve after all, and she went at it with vigor. It was rather nice how much better she felt after.

She tiptoed back out of the bathroom, paused and looked at Gage,

She took advantage of the fact he was asleep to drink in the messy tumble of his curls, the slight part of his lips, the lashes so thick they were casting a shadow on his upper cheek. The man who had saved her life. It made her feel as if there was a bond between them, like they were two survivors of a shipwreck.

As if he sensed her gaze on him, his eyes flicked open.

Other than on the man before her, she knew she had never ever seen eyes like that before, the green-grey snapping with some kind of energy, a force to be reckoned with.

They looked at each other, silent. It lasted a beat too long, and yet it didn't feel as if it had been long enough when he stretched mightily, his shirt lifting to show her the hard lines of a taut belly.

"What are you doing up?" he asked.

"Nature called."

"You could have asked me to help you."

"I don't think so," she said proudly, indignant at the very suggestion.

"You're swaying on your feet."

"I'm not." But nonetheless she did not protest

when he leaped from the chair, took her elbow and gently guided her back to the bed.

His touch felt familiar and appealing and she felt a strong need to deny the appeal. She jerked her arm away and climbed back into the bed.

"What happened to Troy?" she asked.

"He'd been up all night. I came in and relieved him early this morning. How are you feeling?" he asked.

"My head hurts."

"I can see the bandage needs to be changed."

"I'm sure they'll look after that at the hospital."

He didn't say anything. "Besides your head, how are you feeling?

"Groggy. Confused. Embarrassed."

"Embarrassed? How come?"

"Like the rest of my life, last night seems to have disappeared in a haze, but a few humiliating snippets are on this side of the cloud."

"Give yourself a break," he said. "Whatever the doctor gave you could have knocked out an elephant."

Give yourself a break.

Hailey contemplated that. She was fairly certain it was not part of her makeup.

"I sang," she groaned.

"Maybe a little bit."

"Was it awful?"

"Like being serenaded by a cat with its tail caught in a door."

"Thanks for not holding back."

"You're welcome," he said, and the grin he gave her was cheeky and dazzling and made the sparkle in those green eyes deepen even further. It was really not something a woman in a weakened state wanted to be up against.

Thankfully there was a soft knock on the door, and her other rescuer, Seth, came in. "How are you doing this morning?"

"Despite the escaped-from-the-asylum outfit, and the mummy look, pretty grateful to be alive. I really can't thank you both enough."

"Do you remember anything?" Seth asked carefully. "Anything at all? Like how you got to be in the water?"

"Beyond my first name, I'm drawing a blank." She snapped her fingers and shot Gage a puzzled look when he bit back a snort of laughter. "Except this morning when I woke up I was pretty sure I went to college."

"Oh, that's good," Seth said. "Where?"

"I couldn't conjure that information, unfortunately. It seems to have been brought on by a memory of being hungover as a result of college shenanigans."

Another snort of suppressed laughter from Gage.

"Is there something about my situation you find amusing?" she snapped at him.

"No, ma'am."

She gave him a long look. For some reason it felt as if she was quite practiced at that particular look.

She had a sudden flash of a little boy standing in front of her, chocolate smeared around his mouth.

Billy, did you take Betsy's candy bar from her lunch bag?

No, miss.

The memory came and was gone almost as quickly. What good did that kind of memory do her, anyway? Except she knew she loved that little boy, whoever he was, dearly, and that absolutely the wrong time to let him know it was when he'd just eaten someone else's chocolate.

Exactly the kind of detachment necessary to get a straight answer from Gage about his amusement.

"Well, okay," he admitted, "maybe I find it a little bit funny that you think you can snap your fingers and you can't. And also your vocabulary is…er…interesting."

"In what way?" she asked.

"In the four-syllable way."

"I'm surprised," she said. "You don't strike me as the kind of man who would know that much about syllables."

As soon as the words were out of her mouth, she wished she hadn't said them. She had the awful feeling her normal filters had been knocked out of place.

"Oh?" he asked mildly. "What kind of man do I strike you as?

"What I'm trying to say is that you seem more the molding-your-muscles-in-the-gym type than the studying-the-structure-of-words type."

She hoped he wouldn't interpret that as her looking at his muscles.

She remembered admiring them last night as she'd gone up in the elevator. She remembered the smile on his face when he'd caught her at it.

Maybe a little sharpness in her tone was a good defense against this insane attraction to him.

For some reason she knew this absolutely. She had to defend against it.

He was attractive. He knew it. She knew it, too. That didn't mean she had to be under the spell of it.

He flexed a muscle—she was 100 percent sure for her benefit—and then snapped his fingers, and he did it well. It was like a lid being cracked down on a bucket. "Bingo," he said.

"Touché," she said. She suddenly felt contrite that she was being so prickly. She thought, but wasn't at all certain, that it was out of character for her. "I'm sorry. I don't mean to be…"

She searched a mind gone suddenly blank for the right word.

"Persnickety?" he provided.

"Precisely," she said sadly.

"It's okay," he said. "I understand you're discombobulated."

She gave him a flustered look. He seemed to be enjoying a private joke.

Seth looked between them with interest, then cleared his throat. "I've been up all night, and I hoped to have some answers for you by this morning," he said.

She was humbled by the caring of strangers. Troy and Gage taking shifts by her bed, Seth staying up all night.

"Unfortunately, no one has reported you missing yet. I've got people calling hotels to see if they had a guest, first name Hailey, but so far drawing a blank."

"Thank you for trying. I'm sure the hospital will have a few strategies for finding people's identities, as well."

Neither man said anything.

"I'm supposed to go to hospital today—is that right?"

The two men exchanged a look she couldn't quite read.

"Actually, we thought we should talk about that," Gage said.

She cocked her bandaged head at him.

"We wondered if it might not be better to keep you here," Gage said.

This seemed, given the muscles, the attraction and her lack of filters to be an impossibly poor idea.

"Thank you, of course. What an incredibly kind offer. However, I think I've been enough of a nuisance," she said carefully.

It felt familiar—very familiar—to not want to put anyone out. Ever.

Even so, in her own ears her protest was embarrassingly and obviously half-hearted. In her defense, to choose an austere hospital bed in a strange place where it was possible no one even spoke her language or this? It was hardly a toss-up.

Still, she had to have some pride. She could not impose. She tried to inject a little more conviction into her voice. "I will choose the hospital."

CHAPTER EIGHT

GAGE LOOKED AT Hailey incredulously, as if she had chosen a fast-food burger over a meal at a five-star restaurant, which come to think of it, basically she had.

"We do have a qualified medic on board and Gage is something of an expert on head injuries," Seth said smoothly, as if she hadn't made her decision clear.

"Why?" she asked.

"Why?"

"Why is Gage such an expert on them?" She turned to Gage, "You're not a doctor, are you?"

"Good grief, no," he said, as if being a doctor was as unlikely a choice for him as piloting a rocket to the moon. "I'm just the concussion king. The hazards of building muscle in the gym."

There was that mischievous, all-charming grin again.

"Concussions are very dangerous," she said—nothing to grin about—and did her best not to *act* charmed, even if it was nearly impossible not to be charmed by Gage.

"That's why we'd like you to stay here," Seth explained. "They can, indeed, be quite dangerous."

"Hmm," she said, "I didn't realize the gym was hazardous. You can drop the barbells on your own head?"

Seth suppressed a snort of laughter.

"It's all in the spotter," Gage said seriously.

Seth spoke again. "We have the ability, on board, to monitor you pretty closely. It should be twenty-four hours of constant checking for pupil activity, watching for vomiting or nausea, or increasing confusion. After that, we could reevaluate. The doctor was confident you were suffering only temporary memory loss. Maybe you'll be headed for home—wherever that may be—in twenty-four hours. Hopefully, forty-eight at the outside."

It was very sweet how intent he was on convincing her. There was a temptation, and a strong one, to just say yes to what she was being offered.

But then there was a different kind of temptation that felt as if it needed to be fought. And that was—despite her close call, despite the fact she was still woozy—how attractive she was finding Gage. Particularly when he did the boyish grin thing.

That just felt way too complicated. No, it was best to get off this vessel and get on with her life. Whatever that meant.

"Is this your decision to make?" she argued, addressing both men. "This is obviously a privately owned vessel and a very posh one. Who owns it? Won't they have something to say about you fishing strays out of the sea? And keeping them? I mean you don't know anything about me. I could be pocketing the silver."

"That's true," Gage said, looking at her thoughtfully. "Though carrying around pockets of silver might require some exertion, and you nearly fainted from the effort of brushing your teeth earlier."

"I was fine!"

"Uh-huh."

Seth looked between them again, then cleared his throat. "Sometimes," he said, "who people are is pretty obvious, without them saying a word. You seem trustworthy."

"Like Agent Persnickety," Gage agreed.

She resisted the desire to point out that he was speaking gibberish. There was something about the way he shoved his hands in his pockets that made her think he was less enthusiastic about having her on board than Seth was, despite his outward appearance of having an easygoing manner.

Did he feel it, too, then? This mysterious pull of attraction? Did he understand it was a complication neither of them needed at a time so fraught with unknowns?

She thought of the image she had just confronted in the mirror. Gage being attracted to *her* felt unlikely. A one-sided crush—no doubt brought on by his heroic rescue of her—felt like another reason to go ashore. Pronto.

And yet, there was that weakness, wiggling away inside of her, breathing *Stay*. The prospect of leaving the boat with *nothing*—no money, no memories, no phone—suddenly seemed to require bravery, not to mention energy, that she was not sure she had.

"The vessel is owned by a corporation," Gage said.

"Luckily for you," Seth added, "because the kind of rich guys who own megayachts can kind of be jerks."

A look passed between them. Gage's eyes gleaming with laughter, though there was none in his voice when he said, "The corporation that owns it is called Touchdown. Have you ever heard of it?"

Hailey waited to see if a bell rang somewhere in her foggy brain. "Not that I can think of."

Why would he look pleased by that? Or maybe, befuddled as she was, she had misinterpreted the look on his face, because it was gone almost instantly.

"We just think it would be best if you stayed on board until we can get some answers for you," Seth said smoothly. "Hopefully sooner rather than later."

She mulled that over.

And then it struck her. The awful reality was that although this was being presented to her as a choice, she really had none.

"Of course, if you decide to stay," Gage said gleefully, "you'd have to promise not to sing."

Strangely enough, that was what clinched it.

But she wasn't quite sure if it was the fact that he allowed the decision to be hers, or the fact that being teased by him made her feel something that she wasn't quite ready to leave behind even if it would be sensible to do so.

That was interesting. Hailey was certain that she was usually very sensible.

On the other hand, how did a sensible person end up in a predicament like this?

"Meanwhile, I thought if you had any memories, you might like to jot them down," Seth said. "No matter how small they seem, it could be important."

She looked at the notebook he had given her and inspected the pen.

"Sea glass," she breathed. "I just realized I love a good pen. Is this a Levenger? And what does it say about me that I know that?"

"You're a geek?" Gage suggested.

She managed, just barely, not to prove his point by caressing the pen or smelling the pages of the leather-bound notebook.

"Thank you," she said to Seth, pointedly ignoring Gage. "I already have a memory to write in it. Something that came to me this morning."

"And what was that?" Gage asked, sobering.

"I had a memory of being crouched down in front of a little boy named Billy. I asked him if he had taken a chocolate bar from Betsy's lunch bag, and he said, 'No, miss,' even though he had a little smear of chocolate around his mouth." She smiled at the memory. "See? Nothing."

"I don't see it that way," Seth said slowly. "We already know a few things about you. You probably went to college, you don't have any rings on, and there's no indication you've recently had a ring on, either, so I'm going to guess you're not married since he called you *miss.* Maybe you work with children?"

Married?

She felt a certain dread coil in her stomach.

"I think the trick will be just to let thoughts and memories happen naturally," Gage said. "Don't force anything. Just let nature take its course."

But to be honest she was not at all convinced that letting nature take its course around a man like him was a good idea at all.

Seth took his phone out of his pocket. "Do you mind if I take a picture of you?" he asked. "I'll send the crew ashore with it, and they can start showing it around."

She thought of her reflection in the mirror this morning and really didn't want her picture taken, but like much of her life right now, what choice did she have?

"All right," she said, reluctantly agreeing to the picture, and just as reluctantly added, "I'll stay."

After the men left, she tucked herself deeper under the covers, gazed around with wonder and allowed herself to surrender.

It was, after all, a pretty amazing place to land.

"Well," Gage said, coming into Seth's office, "it's been nearly thirty-six hours since we pulled our mystery lady out of the drink. Anything?"

Seth turned from his computer and gave him his attention. He looked exhausted.

"No, not yet. I've expanded my calls to police to neighboring communities, but no missing person report that matches Hailey has been filed. The hotels are cagey about giving out information about guests. I'm hoping they'll be more receptive to that photo. There's only a skeleton crew left on the vessel. Everyone else is in Chania hitting hotels. But they're being very discreet. No media of any sort."

He sighed heavily, then added, "I'm starting to check on vacation and private rentals. It's daunting."

"What can I do?" Gage asked. "You know, besides being a dick?"

"Be careful or your favorite spotter will let you down when you're next bench-pressing two-fifty." He sobered quickly. "Why don't you go talk to her?"

Seth turned back to his computer. Gage could see there was a map of Chania up, with all the hotels and vacation and private rentals highlighted. On a split screen, Seth was building a list of addresses and phone numbers. There appeared to be dozens—if not hundreds—of them.

It was obvious where Gage was needed, and he said so. "What I had in mind was helping you with the phone calls or going ashore with some pictures."

"Oh, sure," Seth said dryly. "We may need media support at some point—as a last resort—but if somebody recognized you, this could turn into a circus. At the speed of light."

Of course. His reality.

"What's the problem with talking to her?" Seth asked. "I've got the crew we have here sharing little things about their lives with her to see if it triggers anything. You could do the same."

Gage was silent.

Seth turned from his computer and leveled a look at Gage. "Are you scared of her?" he asked.

"What? That little scrap of a thing?"

"You seem to have been in hiding since she came on board."

"I have a business to run!"

"Yeah, I bet you're on level 642 of Football 4000," Seth said.

He could protest, but Seth's guess was unfortunately accurate. Except for the level, which was actually 727. Touchdown had developed the hugely popular game.

"You know what I think?"

He didn't want to know what Seth thought!

"She's smart, she's funny and she's cute, and you're terrified of her."

"That's ridiculous," he sputtered. "For one thing, we don't even know if she's married. Or in a serious relationship."

"I'm going to say with ninety-nine percent certainty that's a no."

"I don't think Billy calling her 'miss' or a lack of a ring is enough evidence of that."

"I was more thinking that if she had a significant other, then a missing person's report would have been filed by now."

"Anyway, I'm thinking of *her*," Gage said. "I saved her life. She could have a bad case of hero worship. I don't want to let her down."

"I didn't detect any hero worship when she commented on how many syllables you were capable of stringing together."

"Well, just wait until she finds out who I am."

"You know," Seth said quietly, "she's in a really bad predicament. She needs our help."

He didn't say anything else, but Gage heard the faint condemnation, anyway. He was not, and never had been, the kind of man who turned his back on someone who needed help.

"The real shame in what you've been through in the last few years," Seth said in the same soft tone, "would be if it changed you."

Gage felt the reprimand.

Be a better man. It's not all about you.

"Okay," he said heavily. "I get it."

"Good. Because the Gage Payton I know always ran toward what he was afraid of and not away from it."

"I'm not afraid of her!"

Seth was silent for a moment, and then he said, "I think if I were you, I might see it as an opportunity that she doesn't have a clue who you are. When's the last time you had that? Getting to know someone without having to question what they wanted from you?"

Gage squinted at his friend. Put like that, it sounded not like Gage would be helping Hailey, but more like she would be helping him. He had a prickly feeling of Seth running several agendas here.

"You think I should lie about who I am?" he asked, pensively.

"You already gave her your first name and your last. You already told her the company name. If it didn't ring any bells for her, it's not exactly a lie. If it doesn't come up, it doesn't come up."

Gage left Seth's office and crossed to the kitchen. The chef was there by himself, the kitchen helper having been sent to town armed with a folder of photos. The chef gave him what he asked for without question, even though it was a weird time of the morning for that particular request.

Then he crossed the main salon. The doors had been folded back so that it was seamless between that living area and the main deck. He paused there in the shadows. Hailey was sitting on a lounger, under a shade by the pool. She had on very large sunglasses. The bandage was off her head, and her hair, what there was of it, was an amazing color, like a sandy beach he'd seen once in New Zealand only shot through with gold threads.

He wasn't a man who would consider himself any kind of expert on hairstyle, but hers was terrible, long in some places and short in others, ragged around the edges. On the very top of her head, it still stuck up like porcupine quills. As he watched, she licked her fingers and tried to press the hair down. It sprang back up as soon as she quit petting it.

She had her knees up, and that too-large T-shirt had slid up and was revealing the length of her very pale, slender legs.

She tugged the T-shirt down when one of the crew approached her with a tray and put a drink and a croissant on the round side table beside her. He said something to her, and she laughed.

Gage hadn't heard her laugh before.

It was a pure sound, like water gurgling over rocks. The laughter lit her face, erasing some ever-present wariness and worry from it.

Seth was right—there was something about her he found terrifying. Because if a man pursued anything with her, it didn't feel as if it could be a quick, superficial fling where everyone knew the rules.

That light coming on in her face made him very aware that her lack of memory did not change who she basically was. He hated to admit when his sister was right, but he was suddenly aware how refreshingly different Hailey was from the kind of women he had consistently surrounded himself with.

No hair extensions. Or false eyelashes. No Botox-smoothed forehead, artificially puffy lips. No crazy fingernails, no boob job, no Permatan.

There was something intensely and refreshingly

real about her, and he was shocked by how attractive it was.

When he had first seen her, he had thought she wasn't beautiful. Now, he realized, she was the kind of woman who could make a man redefine what, exactly, he thought beautiful was.

In fact, could there be anything more beautiful than authenticity? Than the essence that shone through even when she had no idea who she was, even when her hair was sticking up and she was dressed in a T-shirt?

On the other hand, he'd been mistaken before. Hadn't Babba seemed like an authentic grandma type? Hadn't he trusted his instincts and been dead wrong?

The problem was, if he was that wrong ever again, he would never recover from it. He felt that at his core.

But it was no way to live a life, sifting through future possibilities, always living in fear of being hurt.

It was certainly not a way to be a better man. He had always set a high standard for himself, and he was being called to that now. Seth was right. He was not a man who ran away from things that made him uncomfortable.

Still, as he moved out of the shadows toward her, he felt like a warrior girding himself for battle.

CHAPTER NINE

GAGE STRODE ACROSS the deck to Hailey and when his shadow fell across her, she looked up.

"How are you doing?" he asked. His tone sounded a little brusque even to him.

"Oh, hello, Gage."

A reminder he probably should have said hello before he started the inquisition.

"Hello."

"How am I doing?" She sighed, and made a vague gesture around her, "Feeling like Cinderella. Look at this. It's stunning. I couldn't have even imagined something like this. A boat with a pool on it? I've somehow landed in the middle of a fairy tale."

Fair warning. Cinderella—and he knew his fairy tales because of his niece—was in the market for a prince. Knight. Cowboy.

And there was something about Hailey—a fragility, a vulnerability, even that wariness—that made a guy feel big and strong and protective.

No wonder Seth had called it. Gage was terrified of her.

"Could you sit down?" she said. "It gives me a headache looking up at you."

He took the seat beside her and handed her the pickle that he'd just got from the kitchen.

"What's this?" she asked with a laugh. "An odd offering first thing in the morning."

"What do you think it is?"

"A pickle, of course."

"That's an improvement," he said. "When we plucked you out of the ocean, you didn't know what a pickle was."

"You're right!" she said, pleased. "And I'll take my victories where I can get them."

"No other memories?"

"I think I live in London."

"Why do you think that?"

"When I woke up this morning, I just felt like I knew that. Not anything valuable like a neighborhood or a house number, though."

Her scent wafted across his nose. She smelled of lemons and soap.

"Have you tried this?" she asked, picking up her drink and taking a long sip through a straw. She sighed with delight.

"I'm not sure."

"It's a smoothie. Made with oranges that were picked this morning and fresh squeezed right on board. Here. Try it."

She passed the frosty glass to him. She was asking him to share a drink with her? Sip from the same straw?

It seemed dangerously intimate. Maybe not as much as clinging together in the ocean, but still…

She lifted up the sunglasses, and he saw the amazing blue of her eyes, watching him.

He didn't know how to refuse. He took a sip. He wasn't sure he tasted oranges. He thought he tasted her lips.

Ambrosia.

He passed the glass back to her. "Pretty good," he said hoarsely. "I like your sunglasses."

"The light bothers me, but I couldn't spend another day in that dark cabin, lovely as it is. They're really good sunglasses. Brody lent them to me."

Brody. A deckhand. Young. Gage supposed he was also pretty good-looking, not that he'd thought of him like that before. It annoyed him that he was thinking of him like that now.

Though it could be pure altruism—she was way too vulnerable to allow one of his crew members to charm her—he doubted that was all there was to it.

"Everyone's so nice," she said, popping the sunglasses back down and leaning back in her chair. "Brody has a girlfriend named Danielle."

Gage was inordinately relieved by that.

"And a dog named Gunther. A golden retriever. He showed me pictures of both. I think he might be trying to get me to remember if I have a boyfriend. Or a dog."

"Do you?"

The faintest shudder went through her. It made

Gage fiercely aware that someone might be responsible for her ending up in the ocean.

He had been a warrior on the battlefield of sports his entire life. He had used his strength to carve out victories, sometimes against impossible odds, to bend that world to his will. But that fierceness existed outside of football, too. He recognized it at his core as he contemplated the possibility that someone might have hurt Hailey.

If that proved to be true, Gage would not want to be that man if and when he found out who it was.

"I don't think so," she said tentatively, "but I don't know for sure. How about you?"

"A boyfriend?" he said matter-of-factly. "Not currently."

Her mouth fell open and her eyes went wide and then he broke and started laughing. "No girlfriend either. No dog. I've considered one, but my sister, Kate, said I had to do a test run with a plant first. If I could keep it alive, then I should consider getting a dog. She even bought me the plant."

"And?"

"I can report that plants perish in about three weeks if not lavished with attention. Or at least a bit of water."

She laughed, and he realized he had hoped she would. Then she picked up the notebook beside her and the pen.

"Are you caressing that pen?" he teased her. He realized he was trying to make her laugh again.

"Maybe," she admitted, then rewarded him with

a chuckle. "Other girls might think being Cinderella involves a ball gown and a tiara, but for me a Levenger pen would be the stuff princess dreams are made of. And Seth just passed it to me as if it was a cheap ballpoint."

"Do you think you *have* a pen like that?" he asked.

Hailey's brow furrowed in concentration.

"I know what it is, but do I own one or only covet one? I just don't know. Do you want to touch it?"

The invitation felt as strangely intimate as sharing a straw with her!

"No thanks," he said gruffly.

"Your loss." She opened the notebook and wrote something down. Her tongue was caught between her teeth with fierce concentration.

"A memory?" he said hopefully.

"Unfortunately, no," Hailey said. "I'm just keeping track of everything."

"Sorry?" Gage asked her.

"The ruined pillow."

So, she remembered that from her first night.

"The smoothie and the croissant. Supper last night. It was steak. Very expensive. Troy brought me a hot chocolate before bed and it came with a mug of warmed milk and the pot of chocolate beside it. I mean it's all unbelievable and wonderful, very Cinderella," she said again with a sigh, "but we know how that story ends."

"Happily ever after?" he filled in cynically.

"I was thinking more of the clock striking midnight, and it all being over. Poof. That's why I'm keeping track of it. So I can pay it all back."

"I don't think that's anybody's expectation," he said slowly, taken aback.

"It's my expectation. Of myself," she said primly. She tapped the edge of the smoothie glass with the pen. "What do you suppose something like this would be worth?"

It occurred to him it had been a long time since he'd known the prices of anything.

"Don't forget to count the squares of toilet paper you've used," he said, deadpan.

"Oh! Thank you for reminding me of that," she said with enthusiasm. For a moment, he thought she was serious, but then she started laughing.

And then they were both laughing. It felt dangerously good to laugh with her.

"I think you're more like Belle," he said when the laughter died down. "And if I was to pick the character I'm most like? Gaston. Me and every other guy in the world."

There, that should be a warning to her.

But she did not seem warned. "Oh," she said, enchanted, "you seem to know the story quite well."

"They had it on at the gym one day."

She gave his shoulder a little slap. "They did not!"

"I have a fairy tale-obsessed niece," he admitted, pretending to hold his shoulder, just to coax another smile out of her. It worked.

"How old is your niece?"

"She's four-and-a-half. Her name is Sarah. She watches that movie over and over again. She has it memorized. Most of the dialogue. Every single song. She drives me to distraction singing."

"What's her favorite song?"

"I'll tell you, but you have to promise not to sing it."

"Don't worry, I only sing when I'm under the influence. I think."

"The one with the dinted teacup."

"Chip!" she said.

He shot her a look. "You seem to know quite a bit about it, too."

"That's true," she said pensively. "I can picture all of it, scene by scene, but not the context I know it in. Tell me about your niece. Maybe that will help me remember something."

He had things to do. He was at level 727 of Football 4000. It was probably darn near a world record.

But he was doing his bit. He was proving he wasn't afraid. He could *help* Hailey. She could get her memory back and disappear from his life as abruptly as she had entered it.

He took out his phone. He *never* did this. He never shared personal information. But if Brody could do it in the interests of helping Hailey, then so could he. He flipped through the photos and passed it to her.

"Sarah's fourth birthday party."

She took the phone and looked at the photo. Her entire expression melted. "Gage," she exclaimed,

"She's utterly gorgeous. Those curls! I see that runs in the family."

She lifted her eyes from the phone for a minute and regarded his hair. "I'm envious," she declared.

He had the renegade and totally unexpected image of her hands tangling in his hair.

That was *so* off mission.

Thankfully, she looked away before his male mind was able to go too far down that track. It was a reminder, that's all. That danger lurked here.

"A *Beauty and the Beast*-themed birthday party?" Hailey breathed. "How amazing. And her dress! It's an exact replica of the ball gown. Where do you even find something like that?"

"Getting a dress like that was a story in and of itself, especially in rural Iowa," he told her.

"Iowa," she said thoughtfully. "You mentioned that before. I'd have to look that up on a map."

"Most of the world would. I don't think you can put that down to your memory loss. That dress was her birthday present," he said.

He didn't add that it had been *his* birthday gift to his niece and that he'd had it custom-made, and his sister had been mad at him for a month.

Kate had called it a ridiculous extravagance for a four-year-old and sternly told him he would have to vet his gift ideas with her from now on.

But the look on Sarah's face had been well worth a month of his sister's wrath.

He leaned over Hailey and couldn't help but smile at the picture of Sarah. He touched the screen and flipped to the next one. The smell of lemons was stronger as he leaned in.

He could imagine his hand in her hair, too. In fact, he wondered if it felt as prickly as it looked.

"That's you!" she said, enthralled. "You're dressed up as the Beast!"

"I am," he admitted. He should have pulled back from that lemon-scented hair, but somehow he didn't.

"But you said you were more like Gaston!"

"She's four. Let her have her illusions."

"You," she declared, smiling at the phone, "are the best uncle ever."

Well, according to his sister that was open to debate.

And then she frowned. "I wonder if I'm an auntie? I would have to know that, wouldn't I? Nobody could forget a beautiful niece like this."

There! A reminder of the mission. His job was to draw memories out of her. "Here's the other little rascals," he said.

Still, even with the mission, he was genuinely enjoying the expression of pure wonder on her face as she looked at his nephews.

"The bigger one is Sam. He's six."

"There's those curls again. He definitely has your eyes."

"My mom—his grandmother—is a little bit of everything: Asian, African and Native American. It's a strong genetic. He's a really cool kid, a team player and supersmart. He started reading by himself when he was Sarah's age."

She glanced up at him, and whatever she saw in his face coaxed that smile out of her again.

"The little one is three. My namesake, Gage. He's a monster. All forward motion, not a single thought goes through his head, always a wide swath of carnage in his wake. The day of Sarah's party, he started a cake fight and made most of the little girls cry by breaking their balloons."

"You adore him," she said knowingly.

"Yeah. All of them." He took his phone from her, and had another quick look at them before he put it away. He found himself sharing a few anecdotes about the family *shenanigans.*

The backyard sleep-out where all three kids had become convinced there was a bear in the yard and run screaming into the house. Sarah losing her teddy bear on vacation and it finding its way back to her. Sam named player of the year on his T-ball team. Little Gage coloring the entire living room floor with his crayons.

"If I had experiences like that with nieces and nephews, I'm sure I'd remember them. I remembered that other little boy, Billy. But it feels weirdly awful not knowing. Do I have sisters? Brothers?" She looked sad for a moment. "What about your mum and dad?" she asked then. "I didn't see them in any of the photos."

He flipped through his phone and showed her a picture.

"Your mother is gorgeous."

"Not bad for sixty-something, eh?"

She glanced at him and smiled at the affection in his tone.

"Are they in Africa? In the picture it looks like it."

"They owned a farm equipment and feed store in Iowa. They're retired now. My mom's determined to trace her ancestry around the world and she's dragging my dad along with her. They're currently in Africa.

"You know," he said, "Iowa is something like eighty-five percent white, so Mom really stood out. She was bullied when she was a kid, but what she got from that was strength and kindness like no one else I've ever met. They're on safari this week. My sister and brother-in-law, Mike, stayed home to run the business."

"But you aren't interested in the family business?"

"My gifts didn't lie in that direction," he said.

"I wonder if I have any gifts?" she said slowly. "I suddenly feel sick wondering if I have a family worried about me, and here I am lazing around by the pool. In paradise."

"I don't think anyone's worried about you *yet*. Seth's made connections with police all over Greece. There's no missing person's report out for you."

"Don't you think someone, somewhere, is worried?"

Was there the faintest wistfulness in her tone? Of course, everybody wanted someone, somewhere, to miss them. And it seemed impossible Hailey would not be missed.

"Your family and friends probably think you're having the time of your life in Greece. Either your memory is going to come back before they realize you haven't been in touch, or they'll eventually realize something is amiss and file a report here."

She looked worried enough. He wasn't going to mention the other dark possibility. That there might be someone out there who wished her harm.

Her brow was furrowed. He wanted to press his thumb against her forehead, as if by erasing those lines he could take her burdens away.

"You'd think I'd have come here with someone," she said quietly. "A friend. A group."

"Hey, it's going to come back to you. All of a sudden." He snapped his fingers. "Like that."

The furrow in her brow relaxed, as if he had made her a promise.

She snapped her fingers, too. "Like that?" she said, but even though she was trying for lightness, she still looked faintly sad.

Maybe that's why he did what he did next.

He sighed. "Let's hope not like that. Somebody has to show you."

"What?"

"How to snap your fingers. I don't know if it's part of your memory lapse or if you really don't know how, but watch closely." He demonstrated. She watched intently, tried and laughed at the failure. Her laughter was exactly what he was looking for.

"I suspect I'm not an athlete."

"I suspect if you think snapping your fingers is about athleticism, you are one hundred percent correct."

He demonstrated again, and she tried again. He watched.

"For heaven's sake," he said, "your middle finger isn't just for flipping the bird. You're using the wrong finger. Here."

And then, he was way too close to her, bending over that lemon-scented hair, and his hand was closing over hers, but he wasn't quite prepared for how small and delicate it felt within his own. He guided the correct fingers together.

"There, try that."

Without being aware of it, she stuck her little pink tongue out between her teeth. He remembered the subtle taste of her mouth on that straw and felt something shocking jolt through him.

"As if you mean it," he said, and she snapped. Grinned. Snapped again. The grin was nearly as potent as her poking her tongue out between her teeth, and made her seem light-infused. He felt intensely aware of knowing who she was, even if she never recovered a single memory.

There it was again. The sense that he could *see* her, and that he could trust what he saw. But it was more than just seeing her. The trust was the component that changed everything, made him acutely aware that his world with her in it would be fundamentally altered. He could see, in diametric opposition to what everyone, including himself, had been sucked into believing—that perhaps it was simple delights, not all the trappings of success, that made a life richer, deeper, better.

He shrugged off the feeling of the world shifting under his feet, and her being the cause of it.

Brody came by. "Can I get you something, Hailey? A refill? Gage, coffee?"

"No thanks," they both said.

When he'd first met the crew, they'd insisted on calling him sir and Mr. Payton, but he just wasn't that kind of guy. He preferred a more laidback atmosphere. He'd quickly dispensed with the starched white uniforms, too. Everybody now was on a first-name basis, except the captain and the officers. The crew wore white T-shirts, just like the one she had on, and shorts.

He looked suddenly at her T-shirt.

"Is that all you've got to wear?" he asked with sudden realization.

"I have a stack of them," she said. "This is the third one I've had on. I changed it up by rolling up the sleeves. Can you tell? Maybe I'll try to borrow a belt from Brody if I'm here long enough to need another change."

She hadn't had a single significant memory yet. Her life was still a blank. He didn't think she was going anywhere anytime soon.

He looked at the forlorn expression returning to her face, and again, felt a compulsion to change it.

Given his shocking awareness of her a few seconds ago, it was probably a really dumb decision.

"I don't think the endless supply of white T-shirts goes with the Cinderella story," Gage said, keeping his tone casual, big brotherly, revealing no awareness of little pink tongues caught between teeth. "Maybe we should go ashore this afternoon and get you a few things."

"Oh," she said, and looked momentarily thrilled with the suggestion. But then her expression flattened out, again. "I don't have any money."

"I'll look after it. On the condition you don't write it down in your notebook."

"But—"

"My treat," he insisted.

And she bit her lip. "Are you sure?"

"Positive," he said firmly.

"What do you do on the boat?"

"A little bit of everything," he replied. "Currently taking a computer program to the next level."

She looked skeptical. "You don't look like a tech guy."

"I said I did a little bit of everything."

She hesitated. "I don't want to be personal—"

Then don't, he thought.

Was she going to ask if he was attached? Did she think the offer he'd made was a date? He needed to clear that up, but before he did, she spoke.

"Do you do okay?" she asked, that little knot of worry back creasing her brow.

At first, he didn't know what she meant. And then

he realized she was asking after his finances. He should tell her what the Belle dress for Sarah's birthday had cost. Or his parents' trip around the world.

It was everything he could do not to throw his head back and laugh, because when was the last time a woman had worried if he could afford to take her out?

No, because of his very public success, there was always an unspoken expectation of unbelievable extravagance from him: five-star dining; flights on a private jet to front-row seats at a Swiftie concert… Then if things progressed, gifts of expensive baubles or perfumes or wines…

Gage realized then he had developed a persona that had nothing to do with who he really was. He played the carefree, generous man of the world. He had so completely given up any idea of ever being loved and accepted for himself that he hid behind all those *things* he was able to provide. He held them up in front of himself like a shield to protect the real person, who still, in the face of all the evidence to the contrary, hoped for more.

For coming home after a long day to kids tackling him and yelling *Daddy.*

For someone whose shoulder you could lay your head upon and surrender your strength, confide your deepest fears and doubts.

For a place where laughter was the only gold that mattered, where wealth was a hand finding yours and squeezing it.

But as Gage's fame and wealth had grown, his

hopes and dreams for a family, for a normal life, felt even more naive and unattainable, but worse, as if revealing them to someone he dated would make him vulnerable in ways that were simply untenable.

Not that going ashore with Hailey was, in any way, shape or form, a date, and thank goodness she seemed to be aware of that.

But he realized, uneasily, given all the yearnings he had suppressed were now suddenly resurfacing in her presence, that Seth had been absolutely right.

Gage had been given a once-in-a-lifetime chance. An opportunity for someone to get to know him, the real him, beyond the persona largely invented by social media, the press, *himself.*

"I'm okay for a couple of sundresses and maybe some shoes," he said. "As long as you don't need Jimmy Choo."

"I don't know who that is," she said.

But whether it was because of her memory loss or her lifestyle that she didn't know the famous shoe designer, he couldn't be sure. He was going to guess, looking at her, a little of both.

"Nothing too Cinderella," he clarified.

She laughed again, a clear, joyous sound that made him aware, as he had been for some time, that his life was missing something.

He hoped it wasn't her. And yet, the smile that wreathed her face was as brilliant as any he had ever received for any diamond bauble he had ever bought.

CHAPTER TEN

HAILEY'S FEELING OF being unanchored disappeared as they took a motorized dinghy from the yacht to the dock.

Now, that other feeling, thank goodness, was back—the one of having been dropped into a marvelous fairy tale. And that sense only increased as she and Gage moved through the streets of Chania Old Town in search of a women's shop.

The city's colorful history—Byzantine, Venetian, classical Greek, Egyptian—were beautifully preserved in its architecture.

Painted alleyways, too narrow for cars, were made even more constricted because of the abundance of plant- and tree-filled containers outside doorways and lining walkways.

Lush vines trailed off the balconies above street level. In some places the bougainvillea on upper terraces was so thick it created bright pink-flowered archways shading the passageways below and casting a pink tinge on the walls.

The structures, rarely more than three stories high, nonetheless created a tunnel-like atmosphere.

Hailey felt as if her senses were so heightened she was almost on overload. Minute and breathtaking detail was overwhelming her: the patterns of the ancient cobblestones in the twisting streets; meandering cross paths; intriguing stone staircases; the incredible array of colors in the buildings; the petals on the flowers that overflowed from window boxes and containers. The warm air, trapped in these tight streets between buildings, was laden with the perfumes of coffee and cooking, flowers and spices.

Some of the streets were slightly wider, and then tables and chairs were set out in the already crowded space. People seemed so relaxed. There was summer holiday happiness in the air as they tasted wines or sipped iced coffees.

Even the birds that flitted about delighted her, hopping around and tilting their heads hopefully at the people sitting at the outdoor cafés.

She was almost positive this feeling of being so incredibly alive—engaged—was because she had been given a second chance at life, and it was euphoric.

Though it also might be because of the man at her side: the way that beard didn't detract from his appearance at all, but drew her attention, over and over again, to the beautiful line of his mouth; the look on his face after they had shared a straw; the way his hand had covered hers when he showed her how to snap her fingers.

He'd been supremely attractive *before* he'd

shared the photos and stories about his niece and nephews, and talked about his mother.

For some reason his respect and affection for his mother had made her feel, briefly, as if she was on the edge of a cliff in the middle of the night, and if she looked over she would tumble into a mouth of darkness.

But the feeling had been fleeting, chased away by that look on his face of unguarded tenderness for his family, a look that had put his attraction so far over the top that Hailey was not sure she had words for it.

That sense of heightened awareness as they moved through the Old Town extended to him: the masculine scent that wafted off him; the easy, athletic grace he carried himself with; how quickly he took hold of her elbow when the uneven streets tripped her up; how his presence alone seemed to part crowds in front of them.

Hailey had made a list of very basic items and it was a little overwhelming how much she needed. Even if her stay onboard the *Seas* was short, she had nothing. The underwear she'd been rescued in had been mysteriously laundered, but she had nothing else. No shorts. No shirts. No dresses. No pajamas. No shoes, except for a pair of spa slippers she'd found by the pool.

She hoped Gage knew what he had let himself in for, by offering to pay, and vowed to keep her shopping Spartan.

Though maybe not quite as Spartan as what she

was currently wearing, which was the too-long white T-shirt. She had borrowed a belt, and done her best to turn it into a simple tunic dress. Her ensemble was completed with Brody's sunglasses, and the spa slippers, so thin she could feel the heat rising up from the street through their flimsy soles.

Gage was wearing crisp shorts, a golf-style shirt with a collar and that football emblem she had noticed on his clothing before. He had on a baseball cap—same emblem—pulled low over his eyes, and sunglasses. Even though, with the addition of the cap and sunglasses, you couldn't see his incredible eyes, she saw people give him long second looks.

"Hey," he said, stopping abruptly. "Do you want ice cream? Look, there's a shop."

She thought, really, she would be spending enough of his money and that they should stay focused.

But he was already in front of the shop looking at the menu.

"The ice cream here is called *kaimaki*," he told her. "It has an ingredient in it—a resin from the mastic tree that grows on the island of Chios—that gives it a really distinctive flavor. You should try it."

She looked at the menu. It was in euros and seemed relatively affordable, but even so…

"I don't want to take advantage," she said.

Even though his eyes were hidden behind sunglasses, she could see by the quick downturn of his mouth that he was annoyed.

Without asking her further, he bought two ice creams and handed her one.

"Don't say one more word," he said to her.

"Okay."

He groaned. "That was one."

"I don't follow instructions well."

"Somehow, I had that figured out already."

The ice cream, with the addition of that exotic ingredient, was scrumptious and faintly chewy, though soon it was melting down their hands in the growing afternoon heat.

Since when had a man eating ice cream been just about the sexiest thing on the planet? She tried hard to just focus on her own, but her eyes kept drifting to him and his beard-framed mouth. What his tongue was doing to that cone should be illegal.

A white droplet caught in the beard, and her eyes fastened there. He caught her looking.

"Beast?" he asked, wiping his mouth with the back of his hand.

It was the smallest gesture, and yet it created a knife-like pang of longing, followed by the feeling she remembered from out in the water.

That attraction was dangerous, something to be fought, not indulged.

"This looks like a dress shop," he said, stopping, and popping the remainder of his ice cream cone in his mouth.

Watching him swallow it with such grave pleasure, it felt that there were some things that couldn't be fought. She stepped hastily up to the window.

There was a mouthwatering array of items displayed there, but again the prices were in euros. This time nothing seemed even relatively affordable.

From the tightening in her chest, she was pretty sure she had just filled in one more piece of the puzzle that was her.

She was poor.

She opened her mouth to protest that maybe this wasn't quite the right store, but he was watching her from behind those sunglasses. His lips twitched in warning. She swallowed what she wanted to say. It was, after all, the first dress shop they had seen.

A kitten, orange and white, and very young, appeared from behind a flowerpot. For whatever reason—perhaps it had caught a whiff of the ice cream—it beelined toward them, crying piteously.

Gage went down on his heels and let it lick his fingers. "Poor little guy. He's hungry."

There was that primal jolt again, watching this strong, supremely well-assured guy going complete softy for a kitten. The jolt was strong enough that it was overriding whatever was trying to order her to be cautious.

Wordlessly, she passed Gage the remainder of her cone and watched as he held it up for the kitten.

For a man who'd said he couldn't even be trusted to keep a plant alive, he seemed to be doing pretty well with the kitten. The tiny creature gobbled down the ice cream, and Gage, smiling, wiped at its now messy face with his thumb. It occurred to her how utterly confident of his own masculinity a man had to be to be crouched in the street making a fuss over a kitty.

"It acts like it's starving," Hailey said with concern.

"Go on in," he said. "I'll meet you in a minute." He scooped up the kitten. "I'll see if I can find where it wandered away from."

The truth was she could stand here and watch that powerful man with that kitten held against his chest all day.

She forced herself to move away and pushed open the door.

The shop was small and exquisite.

A woman emerged from the cool darkness of a back room. She was beautifully and expensively dressed, and perfectly coiffed. A pearl necklace was looped around her neck and diamond earrings winked at her ears.

The woman's gaze went to Hailey's hair, and then she took in the belted T-shirt and the cheap flip-flops.

Maybe it was Hailey's own realization that she was poor—or maybe it was the fact she had to wipe her sticky fingers on her T-shirt—but Hailey was pretty sure that was scorn in the woman's eyes.

And she was pretty sure she had never been in a shop like this before, either.

"Sorry," she mumbled, "wrong place."

She whirled to head out again and bumped right into Gage who was coming in, trying to close the door firmly on the kitten, who was trying to come in with him.

"I have to get out of here," she told him.

"What?"

"I look like a vagrant and—"

He took in the whole situation with a glance and lifted his sunglasses.

"You do not look like a vagrant," he said. There was something stern in his eyes. But also something that said he *saw* her. And then he took her by her shoulders and turned her back around.

The woman's gaze went to Gage.

He returned her look, narrow-eyed, and Hailey realized people did not say no to him. Even dressed ever so casually, Gage radiated composure.

"How may I help?" the woman said, her English accented, her attitude as flipped as if a light switch had been turned.

Gage did not answer for her, but gave Hailey a look that clearly said *Take it from here* and coaxed a smidgen of her own confidence to the surface.

"I have a list," she said. She certainly wasn't going to say, in front of Gage, that she needed underwear!

"I'll be back in an hour," he said. "Just get whatever you want. At least enough for a couple of days. Don't forget a bathing suit."

He turned back toward the door and then stopped. To the snooty saleslady, he said, "Do not let her look at price tags. Am I clear?"

The lady nodded, barely able to contain her glee.

Hailey watched him through the window as he ran into a member of the ship's crew and they paused to chat. She said firmly, "Of course I'm looking at price tags!"

But the woman had clearly decided who the boss was. She held out her hand for the list and introduced herself as Eleni.

"You need everything?" she asked, scanning it and sending a puzzled gaze to Hailey's current outfit.

"My luggage was lost," Hailey said, which was easier than explaining *she* was lost. She looked around the shop and suddenly felt overwhelmed and slightly dizzy.

She realized she was not quite as recovered from her ordeal as she'd thought. She pressed a hand to her forehead.

Eleni, concerned, ushered her to the changing room area and brought her a glass of water. She looked at her, tilting her head, assessing.

"You just sit there. I'll bring things. I know exactly what you need. You decide yes or no. Then, if you're feeling better, you can start trying on."

"The less expensive the better," Hailey reminded her.

The other woman nodded her agreement, but every single item she brought had had the price tag removed.

The lightheaded feeling, thankfully, with the help of the water, passed very quickly.

An hour later, Hailey had to admit that Eleni

did know exactly what she needed. She'd also realized her initial assessment of the woman had been caused by her own insecurity, because Eleni acted as if Hailey was an adopted child.

She brought underwear first. She showed a streak of stubbornness when Hailey tried to make her understand she wanted utilitarian items.

"Not around a man like that," Eleni said firmly.

"It's not like that," Hailey protested. "We're not together."

"You looked like you were together to me," Eleni insisted.

"Well, not in a way that he's going to see my underwear."

"You think you wear underwear like that for *him*? No! It's because of the way it makes *you* feel!"

CHAPTER ELEVEN

ELENI WAS RIGHT, because with every piece of filmy, silky underwear she tried on, Hailey felt more deliciously feminine.

The problem with not having a memory was she couldn't be certain if she'd ever felt quite like this before.

She didn't think she had, as danger signs didn't seem to be flashing inside her brain. It felt as if she was discovering a side to herself that might have gone unexplored in the past that was lost somewhere in a gray fog inside her brain.

After the underwear was sorted out, Eleni trotted out bathing suits. When Hailey rejected the bikinis immediately, Eleni sighed heavily.

"You're young! You're perfect! Enjoy it. It doesn't last forever!"

Nonetheless, Hailey chose a very conservative maillot-style suit in plain black.

Then the clothes came.

Eleni had an absolutely flawless eye not only for sizes but for what looked, not just good, but fabulous. Or maybe all expensive clothes looked fabulous.

Or maybe really good underwear made clothes look fabulous.

Whatever the reason, as she tried on each outfit, Hailey felt as if a butterfly was emerging from a cocoon.

Soon, Hailey had chosen a lightweight pair of linen trousers and a couple of cool, sleeveless summer-patterned blouses—one with flamingos on it—that felt fresh and flirty and fun.

Yet somehow, she was aware fresh and flirty and fun might not be her usual style. At all. She picked two pairs of shorts that seemed a little too short, but Eleni rolled her eyes at the complaint. A pair of canvas lace-up sneakers were added to her stash.

At Eleni's insistence—the woman hadn't been wrong so far—Hailey tried on a Greek-inspired peasant blouse, white, the elasticized neckline pulled down, leaving her shoulders bare. It was paired with a full pale blue skirt with embroidery at the hem. She was just whirling in front of the mirror in it, loving the gypsy feel of the way the skirt danced around her legs, when the front door squeaked open and Gage came in.

He took in Hailey as the skirt floated back into place around her and lifted his sunglasses. For a moment, she thought he was going to whistle, but instead he just nodded his approval. "You clean up pretty good, Polo."

She blushed at the look in his eyes, and it was

somehow gratifying—if perilous—that she wasn't the only one with awareness bubbling away briskly in the background.

"Not together. Sure," Eleni muttered shaking her head. Then, "You have to try on this."

She held one more dress aloft.

Even on the hanger, it was beautiful. It was the kind of dress that women who came aboard the *Seas du Jour* probably wore all the time. It was nearly as filmy as the underwear and seemed to be constructed of the smoke and silver of a storm cloud.

While all the other selections had been young and fun, perfect casual wear for a resort destination, this dress was distinctly grown-up. Sensual, rather than sexy. Sophisticated—the kind of dress a woman might wear to an upscale cocktail party or a very special night out.

"Oh, I don't need anything like that," Hailey said swiftly, even as she recognized a part of her longed for it. But was it a part of her that she used to be or a part of her that she was becoming?

Since she had decided she was poor, she was pretty sure it was the latter.

That, she thought, was the problem with indulging in Cinderella temptations. The time came when they had to be let go.

"At least try it on," Eleni said persuasively. "From the moment you walked in the door, I thought of this dress and you."

So, she hadn't been labeled a vagrant. That was

something she had created, some insecurity that she carried. Hailey felt a little ache start behind her eyes.

A woman's voice in her mind, sharp, said, "*Who do you think you are?*"

"Try it on," Eleni insisted. "Just to see. What you can be."

Hailey shot Gage a look. He lifted a shoulder.

"You specifically said nothing too Cinderella," she reminded him, with a hint of desperation, because it was the kind of dress that changed who a person thought they were.

But she didn't have a clue who she was!

Which, a voice whispered within her, made the canvas blank, ready to be filled in any way the artist chose.

"Take it from me, the reluctant expert in fairy tales—it's more Belle than Cinderella," he said. And then he dropped the sunglasses back over his eyes.

Feeling exquisitely bold—probably egged on by her new underwear—she took the dress from Eleni and went back into the fitting room.

The dress, on, seemed as if it might be constructed of gossamer. It was so light that it skimmed around her as if it weighed nothing at all. The fabric was fine, on the verge of transparency, and it ever so subtly outlined the new underwear beneath it.

It fell around Hailey like mist: perfectly cut, narrow straps at the shoulder, a deep V at the neck, pinching in at the waist before it fell, like a cascade of moonlit water to her feet.

Even with her crazy chopped hair, Hailey felt

completely transformed. She gulped. Did she show it to Gage?

She felt as if whoever she had been before might not have shown it to him.

On the other hand, who she had been before had landed her in the middle of the Aegean Sea, close to death.

Maybe the new her emerging was the art promised by that blank canvas, the ability to create herself.

The door opened and Eleni's arm appeared. In her hand was a pair of sandals, silver and sparkling with diamond-like beads.

Just like glass slippers, Hailey thought, staring at them as if in a trance, before slipping them onto her feet.

The shoes had incredibly high heels. She turned and looked at herself in the mirror.

She nearly gasped. She actually—probably for the first time in her life—looked tall. There was a dreamy quality to her, as if she had been spun completely out of magic and moonlight. All she needed was a tiara, and she would be completely transformed.

She had become what every girl dreams of, if even in secret. A wand had been waved. She was, magically, a princess.

Why not embrace that? It was just for a few seconds. Obviously, even without a tag on it, she knew the dress would not be reasonably priced. She couldn't take it. But she could embrace its enchantment for a minute or two, couldn't she?

Drawing in a deep breath, Hailey stepped into temptation and out the changing room door.

As she paused, she saw Gage had removed the sunglasses and was looking down at his phone. He looked up. His jaw dropped and his expression was completely unguarded.

He gave her a look that a woman who had the confidence to wear the kind of underwear she had on—and this kind of dress—*expected* from men.

It was a look that acknowledged the powerlessness of even the strongest of men.

In his face, for a second, was all of history.

Samson and Delilah

Anthony and Cleopatra.

Napoleon and Josephine.

Edward and Wallis.

Bogie and Bacall.

Something, in that second, altered between them, and in some deeply intuitive way, Hailey knew it could not be put back to whatever it had been before.

He quickly masked the heated awareness that had shown in his eyes and face.

"I changed my mind," Gage said, but he could not completely strip his awareness of her from his voice, which was hoarse in a way every woman dreams of making a man's voice sound. "Cinderella."

In that moment, Hailey might not know exactly who she was.

But she was 100 percent certain who she wanted to be.

"Oh," Eleni breathed. "Of course, you must have it."

If she had her own money, she would probably be willing to make sacrifices for a dress like this. But she would not and could not ask Gage to buy it for her.

"I can't," she said firmly, quietly, on her way back to the fitting room. Eleni looked crushed, but nodded her understanding.

When Hailey emerged, a few minutes later, with her other choices, the smoke and silver dress was back on the hanger, the glass slippers on the floor beneath it.

A little too whimsical, Hailey chided herself, to feel as if a dress could give off a sense of being forlornly abandoned.

She saw Gage and Eleni at the front of the store by the cash register, chatting like old friends.

He was just that kind of person, comfortable wherever he was, even in the heart of a very feminine store. They stopped talking as she approached. Hailey had chosen to wear the embroidered skirt and the peasant blouse, paired with comfy leather sandals.

Her arms were filled with the rest of her choices, and she came and put them down on the counter. She tried not to have a heart attack as Eleni began ringing up the purchases.

"Here," Eleni said, reaching behind her, and plucking a purse off a rack. "You have to have a bag."

"I don't really have anything to put in it," Hailey protested.

But the saleswoman opened it, plucked cosmetics from the rack behind her and put them in.

"Now you do," she said firmly, and when Hailey started to refuse, she held up her hand, insisting, "My gift."

She regarded Hailey, pleased, as if she was the artist who had created her, and then carefully placed two lovely sets of earrings inside the purse, too, one a pair of flamingos that matched one of the blouses Hailey had picked.

"I hope your luggage never arrives," Eleni said.

Hailey laughed. "Why, do you think it's full of horrible things?"

"Ach," Eleni said and shuddered delicately. "Your underwear. Terrible. Maybe okay for playing sports"

Gage snorted but then pretended a sudden interest in his phone, while Hailey gave Eleni a disgruntled look.

"Now go down the street to the place with the supersize scissors hanging on the side of it. My brother. He'll do what he can to fix your hair, and he's expecting you."

Gage gathered up all the bags and nudged the door open for her with his foot.

"Damn," he said. "Still here."

Hailey looked around. She did think she saw a familiar face, the same crew member Gage had been speaking to earlier.

But then she heard the kitten and looked down.

It was pushing determinedly against Gage's ankle and mewing loudly.

"It loves you," she said.

"Or ice cream," he said skeptically.

"Aw, you couldn't find who owned him?"

"I asked around. A couple of the shopkeepers said it was a stray, that it had been hanging out in this area for a day or two, begging scraps from the tourists."

"What are we going to do?" she asked.

"Run," he said in a whisper, as if they had to keep it secret from the cat.

Laughing, they ran though the crowds together, escaping the kitten. They came to the shop Eleni had mentioned. It was a barber shop, but given the state of Hailey's hair, it might be a good thing Eleni's brother specialized in shorter cuts.

Gage opened the door and as they slid in, he cast a look out the window.

"I'm pretty sure we lost it," he said with relief.

A small, swarthy man came out. He did not have Eleni's gift for languages and simply walked around Hailey, eyeing her hair critically and muttering.

"Translation—" Gage said cheerfully "—*getting ready to charge an arm and a leg*."

She was suddenly being ushered to the chair and pushed down in it, then a large cape was shaken out and put around her neck.

Hailey was pretty sure Eleni's brother was swearing in Greek. But, with a determined look, out came a water spray bottle and a pair of scissors.

He spun the chair away from the mirror and Hailey looked at Gage. He was in one of the chairs in the waiting area, surrounded by her packages. It was a little cane thing that did not look like it was going to hold his weight. He sifted through the magazine selection on the table, casting occasional glances out the window.

Checking for his new best buddy, Hailey thought, amused. The cat apparently had not gotten the memo that Gage could not be trusted with living things.

"Are those all in Greek?" Hailey asked him of the magazine selection.

"It's okay," he said, and added with self-deprecating humor, "I just look at the pictures anyway."

Hailey turned her attention to the little bits of her hair falling on the barber's cloth. With a backdrop of never-ending expressions of Greek dismay, her hair came off. There was way more of it than she'd expected. She feared she was going to be bald!

But then, with a satisfied "Ta-da!" the barber spun her around again.

Her hair was stunningly short, a few wisps and few millimeters away from being a buzz cut. And yet, what there was of it shimmered, flashing strands of gold as the light from the window played with it. She realized she really liked it. It had a playful, pixie feel to it.

The close crop of her hair made her eyes look huge, her skin flawless and the structure of her face exquisitely feminine and delicate. Her lips looked like a little bow of pouty sensuality. It was a canvas that she felt eager to play with.

But, as she tilted her head, Hailey suddenly felt dizzy—as lightheaded as she had momentarily felt in the dress store—only this time, instead of getting better, it got worse.

The world grew dark around the periphery of her vision. Then, through a haze, she could see herself standing at a different mirror.

Her hair was long, and thick and lush, and hung to her shoulders. Her makeup was running. Black rivulets smudged beneath her eyes and ran down her cheeks.

She had a pair of blunt children's scissors in her hand. She reached up and grasped a thick strand of her hair. And then she sawed through it until finally she stood there holding that long, long strand, sooty tears running down her anguished face.

Hailey gave a little cry of dismay as the memory froze for a second and then was gone.

Gage dropped the magazine and with startling speed was out of the chair and standing behind her, his hand on her shoulder.

"Hey," he said sharply, calling her back. "Are you okay?"

She pressed a hand to her forehead. "I just felt a bit dizzy for a moment."

"Maybe we should have left this one more day," he said. "Or not done quite so much. Sorry. I should have realized you weren't strong enough yet."

"I'm okay," she insisted, though she wasn't at all sure that she was.

"Can you find her a glass of water?" He asked, but it was an order. The barber scuttled away.

Gage's hand found hers. He squeezed. His grasp was strong and dry. It was the smallest gesture and yet it felt as if she had waited her whole life for this.

It wasn't just awareness of him, an almost primal hunger for his touch, though that was there, too. There was an element just as strong and more important.

Someone had her back.

It confirmed what her heart had known about him from the moment his arms had closed around her in the water.

In a world where you couldn't trust anyone, or anything—

Hailey's headache intensified. Where was this soul-deep bitterness coming from? The jagged shards of cynicism?

It was related to that memory; she knew it was.

The water came and Gage let go of her hand and placed the chilled glass there. She took a tentative sip, and the here and now came into sharp focus, even as she was aware the memory had not disappeared, but just retreated.

She wasn't sure she wanted to have any more memories if they made her feel like this!

"I'm good now," she insisted, taking another sip of the water and then setting the glass down.

Gage looked doubtful, but paid the barber—

from the look on the man's face a very generous amount—then guided her out the door.

There was a café next door, its tables spread out onto the cobblestones, and he guided her to an empty chair, and put pressure on her shoulder until she sat. Then, giving her a searching look, he disappeared into the café. A moment later, he came out with two cups of coffee and a sandwich.

"Eat," he told her.

She didn't think she was hungry until she took a bite of the sandwich. He sat in the seat across from her and looked at her closely as she polished off the sandwich and took a steadying sip of that very strong, delicious coffee.

"I'm okay, now," she said. "Really."

"You had a memory, didn't you?"

Despite his *I just look at the pictures* comment, he was way more perceptive than he wanted people to think. There would be no lying to him.

She nodded, reluctantly. "I did."

"Tell me."

She didn't want to. It felt pathetic. And yet the look on his face brooked no argument.

"I just remembered cutting my hair, that's all. It used to be quite long," she said sadly.

"Why were you cutting it?"

"I'm not sure. All I remember is I was standing in front of a mirror, crying and hacking at it with a pair of children's scissors."

He sighed. "Obvious, isn't it?"

She frowned. "It is?"

"Some bastard broke your heart."

"Oh," she said, "I don't know." She tried to follow that thread, but the headache started to throb at her temples again.

"I do. Guys. What a bunch of jerks we are."

"*You* aren't!"

"Ha. I'm probably responsible for tons of bad haircuts."

"You're not a jerk," she told him. She gestured at the packages all around them, but what she was thinking of was the way he had taken her hand in the barber shop.

He frowned at that, as if he thought he should try and convince her of his jerkiness, but then there was an earsplitting yowling sound. Gage's frown deepened as he pushed back from the table and looked down at his feet.

"Stop that," he said sternly. "People will think I have my chair on your tail."

Hailey ducked and looked under the table. Sure enough, the kitten had found him again. It was marching in and out of his legs, crying incessantly the whole time.

The timing could not have been more perfect. She didn't want to think about that memory anymore. She didn't want to discuss heartbreak with Gage.

She certainly didn't want him trying to convince her he was a jerk!

Look at the expression on his face! Even as he was trying to sound stern, his lips were slanted upward in the nicest smile as he looked at the kitten.

"It probably doesn't speak English," she teased, straightening, "Or else it would have stopped on command."

Gage shot her a look.

The kitten, as if sensing his focus had been removed from it, shrieked as if it was being declawed.

"Sheesh," he said. He bent down and picked it up. Hailey watched as Gage held the kitten in the palm of one hand.

"It's so tiny," she said.

With a wry shake of his head, Gage pulled it in close to his chest. It settled against him, kneaded his shirt a few times, then closed its eyes. It purred so loudly she could hear it from across the table.

The kitten didn't believe he was a jerk, and neither did she.

It seemed in that moment there was no mistaking who Gage really was.

They lingered for a while over the coffee. And then she saw a familiar face, Brody, coming through the crowded streets.

He was pushing an empty wheelchair.

"I hope that's not for me," she said to Gage. "I'm fine now."

"Uh-huh," he said.

"I'm not getting in a wheelchair," she told him in an outraged undertone.

"Look, I'm feeling bad enough for overestimating your strength. Just get in the chair."

"No," she said, and folded her arms over her chest. What was the point of having a beautiful new outfit if she was going to be pushed through Chania like an old woman?

He leaned close to her. "You get in that chair, or I'll break down the door," he said.

She stared at him, confused. What door? And what was with the faint menace in his tone?

He turned to Brody. "She's being very difficult," he said.

And then, she got it. He was playing Beast to her Beauty, the scene where Belle refused to go down for dinner! She tried not to laugh, but a little chuckle escaped her.

"It would give me great pleasure," he said, "if you would do as I asked. Please."

This was, of course, made even more adorable by the fact he still had the kitten held against his chest.

She could not contain the laughter. "You sound just like him! How many times *did* you watch that movie?"

"Three zillion, two hundred billion and twenty-two million," he said.

"In other words, at least six?"

"Exactly. In the interest of not making me feel like a jerk?" He bowed over the empty chair.

She pursed her lips. "But," she told him, "just a minute ago you were trying to convince me that you—and all men—were jerks."

"Maybe you bring out the best in me," he said, and even though they'd been kidding, he suddenly sounded very serious.

But then, before she could read too much into it, he grinned at her and lifted an eyebrow.

"If you get in the chair, I'll give you a kitten," he said.

Her mouth fell open. He held out the kitten. She knew if she took it, she was lost. But who could resist either of them?

She sighed and got in the chair and took the kitten from his hands. It stared at her solemnly for a minute, then wriggled and gave one faint meow of surrender. She nestled it against her and it went quiet.

"You are way too used to getting your own way, Gage Payton."

For a moment, he froze, then cocked his head and took a quick look around.

After his stellar *Beauty and the Beast* impersonation, now did not seem to be the time for him to be wondering who was listening.

But maybe she was mistaken.

Because he relaxed and got behind the chair, taking it from Brody.

She put the kitten on her lap and it curled up, exhausted, but somehow knowing against all odds, it had found its way home.

"What should we name it?" Gage asked, piling up packages around her.

Being pushed through the crowded passageway was not nearly as awful as she had thought it would be. She could feel the pure power of him as he navigated the chair through the crowded streets. She felt looked after. Spoiled even.

"You can't just decide to get a cat," she told him. "It will need shots, and food and litter."

"We already knew I couldn't be trusted with it. Ask my sister," he agreed. "That's why I'm giving it to you."

"I'm a guest on a yacht. I can't have a kitten." But even as she was trying to convince him, she couldn't imagine giving the kitten up, either.

"Hey, Brody," he said, "go get everything we need to have a kitten."

"Aye-aye," Brody said, without asking a single question, and moved off through the crowd.

She contemplated that *aye-aye*. She wasn't exactly sure how the hierarchy of boats worked, but Gage was obviously in a position where he made decisions and others listened.

"Okay," he said. "Now can you name him?"

"Are you sure it's a him?"

"I hate to admit it, but I had a little look under his tail."

"Then it's obvious, isn't it?" she said.

"Call me a dunce…"

"Marco Polo."

CHAPTER TWELVE

"A KITTEN?" SETH SAID and raised his eyebrows.

"Don't even think of making the obvious joke," Gage said.

"The obvious joke?" Seth said, all innocence.

"You can tell the rest of them, too. No kitty jokes." Only he didn't say kitty.

"Hey, you don't need to tell anyone that," Seth said, mildly insulted.

Of course, Gage knew that. He didn't need to tell them how to behave. The truth was—and Seth could see it—that he felt a kind of sensitivity toward Hailey. Protective.

Gage had stopped at his office to check to see if any progress had been made on finding out who Hailey was.

There hadn't been.

The strange thing was he felt relieved that no progress had been made. He was getting intriguing glimpses of who she really was.

Or could be.

He wasn't ready to give that up. He was aware

he couldn't say that out loud and probably not even to himself.

But if circumstances kept her here, who was he to fight that?

There had, of course, been several offers from crew to take the parcels from him, but he had not surrendered them. He had also not been willing to have the wheelchair fight again on deck, so she had walked, with her kitten, to her room.

Despite protesting she was fine, he was pretty sure she fell on that bed the minute he closed the door. If he'd peeked back in, he bet that she and that kitten would be fast asleep together. If the dark circles of exhaustion under her eyes were any indication, he didn't think she'd be back out of that stateroom tonight.

Thank goodness. Even as he didn't feel ready to let go of her, he really didn't know how much more of Hailey a man could handle. Today, anyway. Vulnerable. Sweet. Smart. Not sure of herself.

I look like a vagrant.

Wasn't that the exact moment everything had changed for Gage? When she had turned to run out of that store, as if she wasn't good enough, something had shifted in him.

Dramatically.

He had gone from wanting to protect himself, to wanting to give her every single experience she thought she didn't deserve.

Then she had put on that dress. In that moment, he had been able to see so clearly who she really was.

Or might have been if she hadn't cut off her hair because of some jerk.

He suspected Hailey had seen who she really was, too. And decided against it. By leaving the dress behind.

A man should respect a decision like that.

But he couldn't. Hadn't.

He'd told the shop owner to have the dress shipped to the yacht with the fresh provisions that came on board every morning.

He couldn't believe he had once thought Hailey wasn't beautiful. It felt as if he'd made a mistake about what beautiful was, been lured in by what so many women thought was perfect.

When what was beautiful was someone who could be genuine in a world that was anything but.

"The kitten was an impulse," he said. "My sister says I have impulse control issues."

"Uh-huh," Seth said.

Yes! Impulse control issues. That explained the dress, too. He wouldn't give it to her. Not right away. Maybe when he found out who she was. Maybe when she found out who she was, in every single way.

A woman worthy of good things happening to her.

He'd give her the dress in celebration of that.

A parting gift.

"Besides, she was upset. She'd just had a memory. She was woozy, and I insisted on a wheelchair. She had to be bribed to get in it."

"With a kitten?" Seth said. "It's not exactly your style."

"What's my style?"

"Tennis bracelets."

"The kitten was what was handy."

"What was the memory?"

For a minute, he felt unsure if he should share it with Seth. She had confided in him. It was personal.

On the other hand, what if it held the clue to finding out who she was?

"She remembered cutting her hair. Standing in front of a mirror with kid's scissors and chopping it all off." He hesitated. "Crying."

Seth looked deeply troubled.

"What?"

"Possible new scenario. Despondent woman comes to Greece. Since there's still no report of a missing person, maybe alone. And walks into the ocean. On purpose."

He thought of the light in her eyes and her laughter and the way she had looked in the dress.

About as alive as anyone he had ever met.

On the other hand, how did he know who she had been before? How could he presume to know that, when she didn't even know herself?

Still, he felt a need to believe in her and to believe that was not in Hailey's nature. She'd given him a fight getting into a wheelchair. She wasn't just going to walk into the sea over something or someone. No, in their short acquaintance he could not picture Hailey as someone who just gave up.

"I don't think so," he said to Seth's suggestion.

On the other hand, even if that wasn't true, the thought of Hailey sitting in front of a mirror, crying and cutting her own hair did something to his heart.

He didn't know how long she would be here. But he felt some resolve in him solidify.

He could get over himself and the self-protective mode he'd been in, enough to give this woman who had been found nearly drowned, who didn't know who she was, some happiness while she was here.

Giving her a kitten had been an impulse. He wasn't even sure if it qualified as a gift since it had been a blatant bribe. And giving her a dress some day in the future didn't feel quite right either. Adding a diamond tennis bracelet would really feel so wrong with Hailey, as if he was falling back on the kind of gift that protected himself instead of bringing joy. You couldn't fix feelings with stuff.

But now that he'd thought of her in that silvery slip of a dress, he realized it was already a little more complicated than he wanted it to be, and he barely knew her! Hailey was upending his world and she wasn't even trying!

He wanted to spend time with her. And maybe, frighteningly, that was the real gift. Not stuff. But to give yourself—your time and your energy—wholeheartedly, to another person.

And maybe, like all real gifts, it benefited the giver as much as the recipient.

* * *

Hailey woke up to a crash. She sat up in bed and saw Marco Polo sitting on the shelf below the television set. Marco lifted a paw to his mouth and gave it an unconcerned, somewhat delicate lick.

A vase—probably priceless—lay on the floor, on its side. She leaped out of bed and picked it up. Thankfully, it wasn't broken.

She had fallen into bed almost the minute they had arrived back on the *Seas du Jour* from the shopping excursion in Chania. She hadn't been too tired, though, to notice that the bed had been freshly made, the sheets appeared to have been ironed, and there were fresh flowers beside the bed.

Hailey had woken briefly when there had been a soft knock at the door.

It was only when she saw it was Brody that she realized how much she had hoped it was Gage, but no, it was the delivery of what appeared to be the entire cat section of a pet store.

She had filled a dish with dry kibble for the delighted kitten who hadn't lifted his face from the bowl for a full ten minutes. When he'd stopped for breath, Hailey had shown him a few toys, hidden a litter box in the bathroom and then climbed back into bed and slept instantly.

Now she saw, that despite the plethora of toys to choose from, Marco Polo had spent a busy night knocking things off shelves, climbing the blinds and scattering cat food all over the floor.

In the bathroom, she saw he had shredded the entire roll of toilet paper, and that the floor was silty with the bath salts he had knocked over.

The kitten marched into the bathroom behind her howling a list of demands.

"You've worked up a bit of an appetite, haven't you?" she asked him, and then she scooped him up and locked him in the glassed-in shower enclosure.

Ignoring his piteous cries, she turned to the mirror and was pleased to see that her deep sleep had benefited her, if not the stateroom, which had obviously needed guarding.

Her fixed hair looked surprisingly good, the dark circles had disappeared from under her eyes, and there was a bit of color in her cheeks.

In fact, she felt absolutely amazing.

Still ignoring the cat, who was now flinging himself against the shower door in protest of his captivity, Hailey carefully chose a casual outfit from her gorgeous new stash. She put on the flamingo-patterned blouse and the matching earrings, and a pair of the too-short shorts. The addition of the earrings made her very short hair look like the deliberate choice of a woman who was carefree and confident.

Then she dabbed on a bit of the makeup Eleni had so thoughtfully added to the purchases.

She felt like a brand-new person. Of course, wasn't that what anyone without a memory would be? A brand-new person?

A person who wore short-shorts and the clothing of someone who was happy and maybe even sexy?

She put on the canvas shoes, tucked her notebook and the Levenger pen into her new handbag and put it over her shoulder.

She freed Marco Polo, but only to scoop him up and snuggle him against her chest.

"You're a brat," she told the kitten. She was not going to leave the little feline unsupervised in the luxurious suite!

She made her way up to the pool area and the deck, not quite sure what the protocol was for breakfast.

Gage was already there, sitting at a table. Like her, he was dressed casually. She drank in the wideness of his shoulders, the tumbling curls, the rough beard, and felt a pang of hunger that had nothing to do with food.

He had a laptop in front of him, but he glanced up as she came in, and closed it. A smile played across his lips as she moved toward him.

"You've brought Marco," he said.

Was that what the smile was for? The kitten? Was she disappointed?

"I can't leave him in that room. He was into mischief all night. He shredded an entire roll of toilet paper."

"I suppose you've written it down?" he said dryly.

"Yes! But we have to talk about it. I'm obviously in no position to have a kitten. I don't even know where I live, never mind having a pet. I doubt if you can even bring a foreign kitten home across borders."

"You're right," he said. "He's an illegal alien if ever I saw one."

"Please be serious. I'm not sure a yacht is conducive to kittens," she said, and then with a sigh, "It might have been a bad idea to take him."

"Impulsive," he agreed solemnly. He reached for the kitten, and she passed it to him, watching as it nestled in his lap, and he tickled absently at its ears. The kitten pushed against his fingertips, purring with utter delight.

"Marco DeStructo," Gage said, amused.

She sank into the chair across from him. They made such a compelling picture that it would be easy to lose one's train of thought. "I think what I'm trying to get at, Gage, is if Marco Polo shatters a priceless vase or shreds the linens, who is going to be responsible for that?"

He took the finger that had been tickling the kitty's ears and pressed it into the middle of her forehead.

"Careful, you're getting a worry line right here."

"Because I'm worried!"

He laughed then and removed his finger.

"Look, it's really not a laughing matter."

"I get it. I've given you a white elephant. I should stick with tennis bracelets, obviously. What would you like for breakfast?"

"I don't think we've resolved the issue of Marco Polo."

"I'll take him back. There. Resolved."

She was surprised to find that didn't feel like a solution. He'd given the kitten to her, and now he was taking it back, but she already felt just a little attached to it. Plus, it was from *him*.

"But what will you do with him?" she asked. She realized she was terrified he would say that he was going to put him back where he'd found him.

"Sam's birthday is coming up."

She opened her mouth to say something. Where was he going to keep it until then? It was a boat. How was he going to make sure the kitten didn't fall overboard? Contain it so it didn't get lost in one of the thousands of nooks and crannies in this enormous vessel? Was he going to be responsible for any damage the small creature caused? What if his sister didn't want a cat?

But, really, who had put her in charge of the universe?

"What do you want for breakfast?" he asked again.

"Is it like a restaurant?" she asked uneasily. "Like I can just order what I want?"

"As long as you write it down," he said, and she realized he was teasing her. "I'm having bacon and eggs."

"If I share yours with you, do I have to write it down?"

And then they were both laughing.

"I thought maybe we should stay on board, have an easier day today. Yesterday might have been a little too much too soon."

We.

CHAPTER THIRTEEN

WE.

It was very important, of course, that Hailey didn't read too much into the fact that somehow Gage had become her caretaker and companion. Something in her was singing because he apparently wanted to spend the day with her.

His breakfast arrived. He put it between them. "Help yourself."

The bacon was crispy and perfect, and though she initially hesitated there really was enough food there for two—or more—people. Which was good because Marco Polo demanded his share, and they took turns feeding him bits of bacon from their fingers.

Sharing off the same plate felt as delicious as the meal itself was.

"So what would you like to do?" he asked.

"I thought we were staying on board, taking it easy."

"Well, yeah, but it's not like one of those yesteryear cruises where old people go out on deck and cover their legs with a blanket watching the sea go by."

She thought that sounded quite enjoyable. Apparently, though, that would be his definition of dull.

"What are the options?" she asked.

"Let's see, there's an IMAX cinema, a hot tub, a games room, a gym..."

"Library?" she asked hopefully.

"Lady! This is not *Beauty and the Beast*!"

"Damn it."

"Reading is not a recommended activity after a head injury. And much of what is on offer here isn't, either."

"Such as?"

"The gym is probably out, and some of the other activities are geared to water fun. So there's an inflatable slide we can put out from the top deck to the water. There's Jet Skis. There's tubes that can be pulled behind motor boats."

She shuddered. "I'm not ready to get back in the sea."

"Okay," he said, and his hand covered hers and gave it a squeeze. "Your head isn't ready for any of those activities anyway."

"You know what I'd really like? A tour of the ship. I'm fascinated."

"Are you sure you feel up to it?"

She gave him a look. "Otherwise, prime the old people deck chair? It was bad enough being wheeled through Chania yesterday!"

"I probably shouldn't have said it like that. It would actually be the perfect way for you to spend the day recovering. On a deck chair."

"How about if I let you know if I'm fading," she suggested, "and we can take a break?"

"Done," he said. "Let me get rid of Mr. De-Structo, and then I'll meet you right here in twenty minutes."

"Try locking him in a shower stall," she called after him.

A half hour later, Gage was taking her to the top deck. He told her the *Seas du Jour* was affectionately referred to by the crew as the *Seas Jour.*

"Seizure," he chuckled. "Get it?"

His enjoyment of the corniness of it was 100 percent *guy* and she liked it.

The boat was a superyacht, a term, Gage told her, that referred to any pleasure craft over the length of seventy-five feet. This one-hundred-and-twenty-foot boat was a highly organized floating community with a four-department crew—deck, engine, galley and interior—with the boat captain overseeing all departments, plus the navigation of the ship. It had a permanent crew of twenty-two people.

Gage took her, with obvious pleasure, through the yacht, top to bottom. They started at the operations room where she met the captain and the second officer. The kitchen—on a boat, referred to as a galley—was absolutely amazing, a commercial kitchen like one might expect to see in a big restaurant. She met the staff, two chefs—the head chef and one for the crew—and then looked in awe at the walk-in coolers and freezers. The crew chef informed her, pleased, there were enough supplies on board that they could be fully self-sufficient for up to six weeks.

They bypassed the luxury living quarters because her suite was on that deck, and she had seen most of it, though not the master suite, which she assumed was probably off-limits.

They went below the waterlines into the engine rooms where the chief engineer pointed out how amazingly quiet the engines were and she couldn't help but notice how clean everything was.

There were, of course, things she would not have considered, like a huge laundry room and a garbage storage facility.

They took a brief look at the crew quarters. There was an amazing gym, though looking at that vast array of equipment, Hailey was fairly certain she was not—and never had been—a gym kind of person. The crew also had their own dining room—mess—and a games room. There were twelve two-person cabins, each with bunkbeds and their own attached bathroom.

She wondered if Gage stayed in one of them. Though they were certainly sufficient in every way, she couldn't imagine someone his size sharing those perfectly adequate, but snug, quarters with anyone.

When the tour was over, she was quite tired and they went up to the main deck and settled on loungers by the pool.

A crew member appeared instantly to ask what he could bring her. She ordered the same smoothie she'd had the day before and Gage ordered coffee, black.

"What did you like the most?" Gage asked.

She didn't even have to think about it. What she had liked most was how he'd interacted with everyone on board, and the way they had interacted with him. People lit up when he was around. Well, why wouldn't they? He had a natural ease around everyone, and he was funny and charming.

Since she couldn't tell him that, she said her second favorite thing, "The crew. What an amazing group of people. They're so devoted to what they do. Every single space we went in, people were working hard, inside and out. There were people polishing the railings and scrubbing the sides. I saw one of the crew members reaching inside a vent with a cotton tip."

"Boats are basically hostile environments. Everything the saltwater touches—and it gets on everything, inside and out—corrodes, so a lot of attention is paid to detail. It's amazing how quickly it can get away on you."

"But the thing I noticed is that everyone seems happy, even though some of those tasks seemed like they might be very repetitive and mundane. I didn't detect a scrap of resentment. I didn't hear a breath of grumbling. That one young guy was standing on a deck rail, using a long-handled squeegee on the side of the boat, and he was singing."

"Singing is allowed," he said, straight-faced, "if you're any good at it."

She *loved* being teased by him. "It just seems like it's a lovely place to work. Do you feel lucky to be here?"

"Oh, every day," he said.

"And am I keeping you from your work?" she asked.

"You are my work," he responded.

"Like an assignment?" she asked. She felt put in her place, somehow, for thinking he *wanted* to spend time with her.

"Don't say it like I've been asked to swab the poop deck," he said, and she made a note to herself that he was way too good at reading expressions.

"Is there a poop deck?" she asked, making her tone light, trying to hide her ridiculously hurt feelings.

She was not sure he was fooled but obviously was as eager to move on as she was.

"A good place for DeStructo!" he declared. "A poop deck."

And then he pulled out his phone and tapped something in.

"Just for future reference," he informed her solemnly, "because this is the kind of thing you might need to know when you least expect it, but a poop deck is a partial deck at the rear of a ship, usually a sailing ship. It comes from the French *poupée*."

She smiled at his over-the-top accent.

"I suppose you speak French?" he asked, lifting his eyebrows at her.

"Not that I know of, but perhaps it will come to

me. Wouldn't that be wonderful? If I got my memory back and I spoke French?"

"Try it, just in case it triggers a memory of fluency in other languages," he encouraged her, and sounded it out very slowly. "Poo-pay."

"Poo-pay," she repeated obediently.

"Any memories?"

"I'm afraid not."

"Still, your accent was very good," he said approvingly. "Now, let's use it in a sentence. Like this: *I hope DeStructo isn't having a poo-pay in my room.* Top that."

"I don't think I can," she said, choking on laughter.

"Poo-pay actually doesn't mean what you think it means," he told her, putting his phone away, and grinning at her, "It means stern."

"Good," she said, "because you're going to have to be very stern with Marco Polo if he poo-pays in your room."

Then they were both laughing, giddily, like children who had shared a naughty joke.

Of course, she didn't have many memories, so how could she know she'd never been around someone like this before?

So at ease with himself? So confident? So naturally funny? So physically imposing and so boyishly charming at the same time? You'd think just being on the boat, surrounded by all this opulence, would make a person feel slightly self-conscious or less than, but it didn't seem to have that effect on Gage at all.

"You want to see a movie this afternoon?" he asked. "We didn't see the theater on our tour."

"Is that part of the assignment or will you get a bonus?" she asked, a little more testily than she'd intended.

"Yes, I'm getting a bonus for luring you to the movies. Buttered popcorn. And red licorice twists." And then he took her hand, bowed over it and kissed it elaborately, "Not to mention the opportunity to spend more time with you, *mademoiselle*."

He pronounced it *mad-dem-mo-sill*.

It was funny. He was kidding her along. So why did the feel of his lips linger on her hand like a brand?

"*Oui*, to the move-ay."

He fished his phone out of his pocket again and pretended to be concentrating on making notes. "The *mad-dem-mo-sill* of great mystery speaks some French. But she will have to decide on a move-ay. I'll look up some choices. Action?" he said hopefully.

She wrinkled her nose.

"Geez," he grumbled, "you don't know your last name, but you know what movies you like?"

"Weird, I know."

"I'm going to guess horror is out."

"I'm going to second that guess."

"Okay," he said, putting away his phone, "I'll surprise you."

The theater room was next to the closed door of the master suite she had not seen. Though perhaps the luxury of the yacht should have prepared her, it was quickly apparent it was more than a room. It was a theater in miniscale, complete with a lobby with a ticket booth and a concession.

A girl in a candy-striped apron took their orders for popcorn and soda. And red licorice twists.

"I don't get it," Hailey whispered. "Does she just stand there hoping someone will come?"

"Of course not. She was notified the theater would be in use. She'll run the equipment and the lighting and stuff, too."

"Gage," she said, with a heartfelt sigh, "I am getting really spoiled."

And then they went through the red velvet curtain into the theater and her feeling of being spoiled intensified.

Because while it replicated an old theater from a different era, it only had about forty seats in it.

And they were not uncomfortable fold-down theater seats, but deep leather recliners. They took seats next to each other.

She dipped into her popcorn and sighed. "You don't even have to request extra butter," she said to him. Plus, it wasn't a date, so she didn't have to worry about holding hands with buttery fingers.

Strange, again, that she would know about dates and buttery fingers, but not her own last name.

They settled and the lights went dim. *Mamma Mia* opened. Did he have to be so sweet? Rescuing

Marco Polo? Picking a movie he thought she'd like? It was bad enough that he was so attractive. Did he have to be kind to animals and thoughtful to boot?

She tried to focus on the movie. She knew she'd seen it before, but had she felt like this? The unfolding themes, a mother's love, a daughter searching for her father, for who she was—

She had a sudden memory of bolting from the theater the first time she'd seen this. At just about this point.

And then of someone being with her. Not a man. Stroking her hair, saying, *Hey, it's not real. It's meant to be funny.*

Hailey's hand went to her throat. A necklace was missing.

"What's wrong?"

"I don't know."

He twisted in his seat and made a motion and the movie stopped. The lights came up. He gazed at her. "Are you okay?"

"Was I wearing a necklace? When you found me?"

He thought about it. "I don't think so."

"It's on a gold chain, with a half heart and some words. Best Friends Forever," she said. "I never take it off. I'm sure of that. My girlfriend and I both had them."

She was trembling, and he lifted the divider between the seats. It occurred to her, crazily, that the seats were designed to be solo *or* for cuddling.

"Hey," he said, snuggling in close to her, and

putting his arm over her shoulder, "it's okay. Just relax. See if anything else comes."

It wasn't exactly cuddling.

And yet his touch, his nearness, the scent of him, the calmness in his voice all soothed her. She closed her eyes and *knew* something.

"Growing up," she said, "it was just me and my mum. I didn't know who my father was, just like Sophie, in this movie. Only it wasn't funny and it wasn't a game."

She suddenly knew, painfully, who the *Who do you think you are?* voice belonged to.

"My mother wasn't anything like the one in the film, either." Well, except maybe for the part where she slept around.

But she already regretted saying as much as she had, as if she had let slip things that were shameful, revealing the real her, something tawdry and awful.

She remembered him talking about his family yesterday. Different worlds. Such different worlds.

And she was increasingly finding him compelling. In fact, at this very moment, if she could think of a way to kiss him, she would. But wouldn't that be the worst possible motivation? To distract herself from the powerful and painful feelings she was having.

Besides, who did she think she was? Just like her mother, probably. She could suddenly picture her mother, beautiful *but* radiating bitterness at the world. And at her daughter.

"You want to try a different movie?" Gage asked gently.

Yes, anything to have the lights dimmed again, so he couldn't see her memories that were on a collision course with the silly hopes and dreams that probably shone in her eyes every time she looked at him.

The second movie was *Beauty and the Beast.*

Absolutely the wrong movie for someone who was trying not to have unrealistic hopes, who suddenly knew she had been raised in a world that did not believe in wishes coming true.

But the movie did what the best stories do: it transported her away from that hard slice of memory, and, of course, she enjoyed every moment of it.

Desperately. Pathetically. Completely.

CHAPTER FOURTEEN

GAGE WALKED HAILEY out of the theater and back to her room. He felt weirdly like a sixteen-year-old boy walking his date home on a summer night and pausing at the front door, wondering if there was a dad peering out from behind the front window curtain.

She'd said there was no dad in the picture, and she couldn't even watch a movie that poked fun at the concept of not knowing who your father was.

It made him ache for her.

Wait a minute.

He'd never really been *that* guy—despite all his mother's efforts to make him considerate and thoughtful—he had not been the one who'd walked the shy girl home or had ached for other people, either.

He'd never been the kind who went for the intense, serious girls who required more of you than you wanted to offer because your focus was on football.

Still, he was aware, standing with Hailey now, that his sister had been right in her criticism of his relationship choices. He had missed something by consistently protecting himself, hooking up with women who required nothing of him but a limitless credit card.

Because he had never once been with anyone—man or woman—who, when he'd asked them what they liked best after a tour of the *Seas*, had said, *The people.*

And being with someone like that required more of him. Terrifyingly, he could feel himself rising to the challenge of that.

The pause outside her door was just as awkward as if they were two kids. This was new territory for him. He looked at her lips.

No, he told himself and was appalled he would even think of it. Acknowledging the deeper, more sensitive self that he had so long kept hidden meant he had to take into consideration her memory loss. There was an implication of innocence with that, which made it unfair to ask her to make a very adult decision.

Even if the way she was looking at him didn't seem exactly innocent.

Her eyes were smoky with sensuality. He could picture himself stepping in closer, tilting her chin up to his, tasting the small bow of her mouth.

But then she took the decision from him. She went up on her tiptoes. She leaned toward him.

He might have closed his eyes.

He might have puckered up.

Her lips brushed against his cheek, above his

beard, and he snapped his eyes open and put his lips back into a firm line. Thankfully, her eyes were closed as she drew away from him.

The look on her face was dreamy, as if a kiss on the cheek was an act of unmitigated boldness.

When she blushed as if she had slipped him her tongue—a red-hot thought if he'd ever had one—Gage congratulated himself on his self-control. It was just a *thought*.

But maybe thoughts had power, because gazing at him, she tilted her head as if she could read his mind. A look flashed through her eyes that made him think she wasn't exactly thinking pure-as-the-driven-snow thoughts, either.

But when she spoke, her voice was prim, a contradiction to the fire in her eyes.

"Thank you," Hailey said, quite stiffly formal, "for a really nice day."

"No, thank you for not making me sit through *Mamma Mia*."

"But *Beauty and the Beast* for the seventh time," she reminded him.

For some reason, it meant something to him that she had remembered what he'd said to her about the number of forced viewings he'd had of that particular movie. A woman who cared about people. And who actually listened.

She was getting dangerouser and dangerouser.

"Well, at least you didn't sing."

That smile drew his eyes back to her lips.

Go inside right now, he begged her inwardly,

or I'm not sure I can be responsible for what happens next.

"Please say good-night to Marco Polo for me."

And then she was gone, the door shut with a firm snap behind her.

He didn't go to his own stateroom, the master suite next to the theater, the one he had deliberately not included in the tour of the boat, because he either would have had to pretend it wasn't his—in other words deceive her—or come clean.

In a way, he'd been deceiving her so far, but it was obfuscation. There had been no out-and-out lies.

Even though he thought now was as good a time as any to attempt Level 728 of Football 4000, rather than face the complexities that were starting to bubble up in his life, he made his way to Seth's office. Gage was aware of a certain dread, rising like mist off lake water, inside him.

He hoped Seth hadn't found out who she was. Because as soon as they knew, it was over.

Whatever was unfolding between him and Hailey would be finished as abruptly as it had started. There was a seesaw within him. Part of him wanted to know where it could go, and another part most certainly did not.

"Anything?" he asked Seth, slipping in his office door.

Seth looked exhausted. Was it Hailey noticing how hard people worked for him that made him notice that?

"No, nothing."

"When's the last time you slept?"

"Ah, it's overrated. Are you finding out anything?"

"Not really, though she is starting to have more memories." He told Seth what had happened during *Mamma Mia*, and about the missing necklace. "Best Friends Forever with a heart on it. From her girlfriend."

"What kind of girlfriend?" Seth asked.

"Not that kind." Gage knew what he'd seen in her eyes as they'd said good-night. "But what if she came on a trip with someone else?"

"Who should have reported her missing by now if she didn't go into the ocean with her?"

"Exactly."

"I'll check," Seth said.

"It can wait," he said gruffly. "Go get some sleep."

For a moment, Seth looked mutinous, but he'd spent long enough in the military that he knew an order when he heard one.

Gage, himself, did not feel the least bit like sleeping. He was well aware that the mysteries around Hailey didn't seem to be resolving. They seemed to be getting more complex instead.

A perfect match for the jumble of complex feelings he was having about her.

But of course, he had the perfect solution.

"Football 4000, Level 728, here I come."

As it turned out, Mr. DeStructo had other plans.

Because naturally, not being as good at taking suggestions as he was at giving them, Gage had let the kitten have the run of his suite for the day.

When he opened the door, it looked as if a land mine had gone off.

And it had the distinct smell of poo-pay.

Gage was already on deck, sitting at the breakfast table, when Hailey came up the next day. The kitten was with him, chasing a feather he had on a string.

He sensed her watching him and turned those amazing eyes on her.

He was casting a spell on her. Last night at her door she'd had to quash an impossible desire to kiss him.

To keep him from guessing her preoccupation with that, she got down on her knees and tapped her fingers at Marco Polo. He attacked with vigor, and she jumped back, laughing.

She glanced up to see Gage laughing, too. He looked tired, though.

"Did you not sleep well?" she asked him.

He lifted a shoulder. He pointed an accusing finger at the kitten. "He thinks nighttime is playtime. I tried your suggestion of confining him in the shower. He cried until I let him back out."

There was something very endearing about such a self-possessed man being taken hostage by a tiny kitten.

"Did you sleep well?" he asked.

"I did. I didn't think I would, because I had some more memories."

He lifted an eyebrow at her.

Had she always thought men who could lift one eyebrow, independently of the other, were unreasonably sexy?

Sean Connery could do that, couldn't he? How on earth did she know who Sean Connery was? She had a fleeting, embarrassing memory of maybe discussing double-oh-seven with Gage that first impaired night.

"My friend's name was Bethany."

"Was?" he asked, alarmed.

"I just meant past tense because I can recall some kind of falling-out that I don't think was recent. There's a terrible feeling of loss around it. On the more productive side, I can remember all kinds of things about her from when we were schoolgirls, growing up in London."

"Progress," he said. "See? It's coming back."

"More slowly than we hoped, I'm sure."

We. Two tiny letters. Such a big word, somehow, connecting people. She looked away from him, over his shoulder, out to sea.

She took in their surroundings.

"We've moved," she said, startled.

"Yeah, we moved overnight. That's what boats do."

"Why?"

"Kidnapping a fair maiden," he said, wiggling his eyebrows at her. "And her kitty."

He said *kitty* very wickedly, but then looked abashed with himself. "Actually the crew hasn't had a day off for a while, so we moved just offshore of a small island that's supposed to have beautiful beaches. Pink sand, very much like Elafonissi, which is famous for it."

"Pink sand," she said, hearing the wonder in her own voice.

"You want to come to the beach with us?" he asked.

Nothing in the world could have made her say no.

CHAPTER FIFTEEN

IN AN HOUR, her bathing suit now on underneath casual shorts and a top, Hailey met Gage on the lower deck, the one she had been brought aboard on that first night.

"We can go in by dinghy, or if you feel up to the Jet Ski, we can take that."

There was that wonderful, complicated *we* again, and it made her brave enough to say yes, even though some of her fear of the sea remained, especially on something smaller like the Jet Ski, where she might fall off.

On the other hand, it was daylight. There were plenty of people around. They had powerful machines. And, of course, she was with him.

Hailey found herself on the back of a Jet Ski, with her arms wrapped tightly around Gage. It was the most physical contact she'd had with him since the rescue, and she snuggled into the back of his body with a sense of homecoming. It was exhilarating being pressed closer and closer to him, baptized by sea spray and bouncing over waves.

The beach they landed at was completely deserted. It really was pink sand, like something out of a dream.

In several trips the crew brought coolers and a barbecue and all the beach toys that she had noticed neatly stowed when she'd first arrived on the *Seas du Jour.*

Within minutes they had set up umbrellas and chairs and a volleyball net.

She wasn't sure if all Americans were like this or if it was just the crew of the *Seas du Jour*, but these people made having fun an art.

They started the morning by choosing volleyball teams, picking straws to see who got to choose first. Gage was the captain of one team and Brody the other.

"I pick Hailey," Brody called when he won first pick.

She went across the sand to him. "I should warn you," she said in an undertone, "I've never been picked first for a team in my life. Actually, I'm usually dead last."

"Hey! You've remembered something," he said, and then called out her recollection to Gage, who smirked as if he might have already guessed that.

Why couldn't she have some nice memories instead of ones that made her feel inadequate?

"He'll take it easy on us if you're on our side." He glanced at her, and added, "Because of the head injury."

There was no need to clarify who *he* was, and that it wasn't all because of the head injury.

Indeed, when she looked back Gage had folded his arms over his chest and was glowering at Brody as if he'd deciphered the young man's strategy.

Brody grinned cheekily at him.

Then, teams chosen, everyone took off their shirts! She hesitated, and then shucked off her shorts and her top to reveal the bathing suit underneath.

It was beach volleyball after all, and at least her suit wasn't even like the ones she had seen the women wear in the Olympics.

The games that followed were not like anything out of the Olympics. They were hysterical. No one took it seriously. Both teams basically played around her, meaning her team was handicapped as if they were really a person short.

But it soon became evident that Gage could have won if he'd been on the other side all by himself.

She wasn't sure she had ever seen such stunning athletic prowess. Gage was in a league all by himself—pure power, and with an unbelievable ability to shift directions, to leap, to propel himself backward.

He spiked with such strength he could put a grown man on the ground if he was foolish enough to get in the way.

But to her, he tempered his incredible strength, lobbed the ball her way, making sure she could get her hands on it. At one point, Brody stooped down, and she rode on his shoulders, guarding the front of the net.

Did Gage look faintly annoyed? Jealous, even? She hoped so.

Then the games were over. Her team had won several with dubious scorekeeping methods and much arguing over the rules, and they chose her as most valuable player, and they had ridiculous trophies they gave out.

Hers was a kewpie doll with a gargoyle face.

She lifted it above her head and shouted, "Thank you to my fellow players for this great honor. I will cherish it forever. And to the losers, I would like to say, keep trying. Never give up. Someday, with work you may—"

Midsentence, Gage barreled down on her, picked her up and slung her over his shoulder. While she pounded his back with her trophy, he ran effortlessly through the pink sand and out to his knees in the water. She braced herself, but instead of tossing her, he put her down and splashed her gently.

She splashed him back and soon the water fight was on.

Finally, exhausted, slightly sunburned and happy, they retreated to blankets under sun umbrellas. Gage flopped down on the blanket beside her.

"I can't believe we have this beautiful beach to ourselves in the middle of tourist season," she said.

"Oh, I think that was probably arranged."

"A private beach?" she said, incredulous, "for a crew party?"

"Exactly," he said. "Loud and rowdy, so don't want to give Americans a bad name."

"I don't think a volleyball game would do that."

"Speaking of that volleyball game, I don't want you to let that trophy go to your head," he warned her.

"What? I was going to see if there was a spot for me on an Olympic beach volleyball team."

He groaned. "Somebody has to tell you," he said.

"Yes?"

"To go along with your singing abilities, you are the world's worst athlete."

"You know, I may not have any memory, but I have a sneaking suspicion I've heard that before. You, on the other hand?"

"Yes?"

"Slightly above average."

He laughed loudly, and she laughed with him. Then he squinted at her.

"Did you put on sunscreen?"

"Oh! I totally didn't think of it."

He casually reached over and slid her bathing suit strap over. She looked down at the white stripe he had revealed. And then, without a word, he got up and went though some of the boxes of supplies they had brought and came back with a tube of sunscreen.

He handed it to her.

When she couldn't reach all the spots, he took it from her, pressed a glob onto his hand, and went behind her.

With all that incredible strength but tempered,

the same way it had been in the volleyball game, he smoothed the sunscreen onto her back.

She may not have had much in the way of memories but a woman just *knows* some things, and she knew being touched like that felt like the most erotic experience of her life.

When he was finished, he tossed down the tube of sunscreen, got up and walked away. Was it so she couldn't see his face?

A few minutes later, he came back bearing hot dogs. He had four of them.

She thought she had tasted hot dogs before, but it turned out no one knew how to do them like Americans.

Still, she could only eat one. Gage polished off the other three. She dabbed a little blob of mustard from his beard. Let's face it—she had been looking for an excuse to touch that beard, and it did not disappoint. His facial hair was soft and springy, a delight beneath her fingertips.

Touching it brought sizzling awareness. She dropped her hand as if she had been burned.

"Are they going to play volleyball again?" Hailey asked him, focusing on anything but him, and the hard beating of her heart, as she noticed teams forming again.

"Yeah, probably all day."

"I'm out. But you go ahead."

"I'm good."

"Because I'm your job?" she said rather pointedly.

"Nah, I kind of like hanging out with you."

For some reason that was more sizzling than him applying sunscreen, than her touching his beard. He flopped back on the blanket and so did she.

"Tell me about your family," she said wistfully, and then hearing the almost pleading note in her voice, she added, "To help me get my memory back."

"Where should I start?"

"Your parents."

She glanced at him. A smile ticked across his lips. "My sister and I call them the Bickersons."

Somehow, she'd been hoping for a fairy tale. "They fight?" she asked, appalled.

"No, I wouldn't call it fighting. It really is just bickering, like she'll remember a trip and say a date, and he'll say, you're out by a year. Or they'll argue about who starred in a film or sang a song. She'll tell him to put the seat down on the toilet and he'll tell her to leave it up. That sort of thing."

She laughed.

"It's funny. I used to see it as a bad thing, embarrassing if they did it in public or in front of my friends, but now I see it totally differently. They have given each other permission to be totally themselves in their relationship. There's no dishonesty between them. They don't ever pretend the other person is right, just to keep the peace, and they don't ever act as if they're happy when they're not. And when it counts, they're a totally unified front. They just have this solid love and respect for each other."

"Go on," she murmured.

"Every year my dad bakes my mom's birthday cake. From scratch. He started it the first year they were married, and they were terrible to begin with. I know, even though I wasn't there for the first ones, because they have a photo album just for that. On one page is a picture of the cake and on the opposite page is the recipe and my mom's rating on appearance, flavor and presentation, like it was the Olympics or something. She was honest, as always. The first cake she gave a minus ten. The first five years those cakes were all pretty bad—flat, lopsided, falling over, icing all over the place. But every year they got a little better. See?" he teased. "Your singing may not be completely hopeless."

She gave him a little smack on the arm for that. "Keep telling me about the cakes."

"Are you remembering something?"

She was not. She just *loved* hearing about it.

"He went through a phase where he did challenging cakes, like tiramisu and Black Forest and Baked Alaska. When I was a teenager he went elaborate for a while, making cakes that looked like things. A vintage car, a turtle, a treasure chest spilling candy out of it. She's given him some high scores, eights and nines, but she's held out on that ten. Now, he's baking more simple cakes. Last year it was just chocolate. Dad's getting forgetful sometimes, and he forgot something—maybe salt—so it tasted a bit off. Might be the first lie my mom ever told him, because she gave it a perfect ten."

Hailey was totally in love with his parents.

"You know," Gage said softly, "when they go, that's the one thing I think my sister and I will fight over—the cake book. Though I think her husband, Mike, would like to burn it."

"Why?"

"Guess what her expectation of him was?"

"He has to make a cake on her birthday?"

"He does. The first year he tried to cheat with a cake mix. That got him like a minus one hundred."

"And now?"

"They've been married eight years. He finally got out of the minus territory last year with an orange sponge cake."

"And when you get married?" she asked softly.

He drew in a sharp breath and glanced over at her. "I'm pretty happy the way I am," he said. "I don't see that changing."

"But if you did," she pressed, "what kind of cake would you make?"

"Ha. A cupcake from the bakery with a candle in it."

She had that slightly nauseous feeling that she was beginning to understand came with a memory.

And there it was, a little girl with long hair and sad eyes sitting in front of a cupcake with an unlit candle on it. Like a camera zooming out, the frame went wider, and the complete picture was revealed to her. A wine bottle on its side on the table, a woman flopped on a sagging couch with her hand flung over her forehead.

She knew that was her mother.

"You've remembered something," he said softly.

"A cupcake just like the one you described," she replied. "It's not helpful. It's not recent."

"How old were you?"

She consulted the memory, but it was already gone. "Maybe eight?"

"Were you by yourself?"

"No. My mother was there. Sleeping on the couch."

He drew in his breath as sharply as he had when she had foolishly ventured into the subject of marriage.

He sat up on his elbow and scanned her face. She tried to look impassive, but she could see he understood immediately that her mother was not really sleeping.

"I'm sorry," he said quietly.

"Thank you."

"Tell me something else about your childhood," she said. "Please."

She could hear the wistfulness in her own voice, so she added, "Maybe it will help me remember something."

He was thoughtful for a minute. Then he said, "When I was in the fourth grade, I opened my desk one morning, and somebody had put a note in there with a racial slur on it."

"Oh, Gage!" Still, she suspected he was telling her this so that she knew every childhood had its challenges.

"It was the first time I'd had anything like that happen to me. My mom had kind of paved the way for acceptance a long time before I came along. It had never occurred to me I was any different than anyone else. So I knew it was this new kid in our class, Ralph. I could tell because he kept sliding me looks and snickering.

"I didn't do anything. I took the note home and showed it to my mom. I told her who I thought it was, and she got a look on her face. She spearheaded this committee that anonymously gave groceries to some of the town's neediest families, and even though she didn't say a word, I knew that she recognized the name. So, she says, '*Meet it with love, Gage*.' I was nine. I took that to mean do nothing. Anyway, my dad overhears the conversation and he takes me aside and takes out a big black felt pen and writes L-O-V-E across my knuckles, and he mutters, '*Meet it with love, all right...*' The next day, I saw Ralph in the bathroom. I told him what my mom said, and he kind of snickered nervously, and then I told him what my dad said and showed him my knuckles. I was already really big for my age, and he was small. He wet his pants."

"Oh, no!" Hailey said.

"Here he is, the new kid in school, and he's wet himself? I mean, his life would have been over, basically. So, I told him to hide and went to the lost and found and got him some pants, and he changed, and we were the best of friends after that.

"Which kind of shows how my dad's approach to life and my mom's worked together to help me."

Hailey felt deeply moved by the story. It also made her feel an incredible warmth toward Gage.

"About the same time, my grandpa, who had started our family store, started to have some odd things happen. A memory lapse here, a fight with a customer there, a really inappropriate remark now and then. It was five years before we found out he had dementia. By then he'd nearly bankrupted the business."

She knew he was telling her these parts of his childhood for a reason. It was not to help her remember her own, but to let her know everybody went through difficult stuff. She appreciated the depth and sensitivity of the gesture so much.

"In the next five years he went from being one of the town's most prominent citizens to being caught shoplifting and forgetting to wear pants. Those were really tough times for us." He hesitated. "And now, I think I see signs of it in my own dad."

With each of his stories, he gave her parts of himself; he gave her the ingredients of what had made the strong, confident man he now was.

And when he'd finished talking, somehow they were holding hands, lying back in the sand, and there was a bond between them, a connection, that had not been there before.

Hailey felt the most exquisite tenderness for him. She had the stunning thought, *This was a man you could fall in love with.*

Finally, he said, "You know what they say?"

"I don't."

"That it's never too late to have a happy childhood," he told her firmly.

It was as if he was intent on giving her that, like a gift, for the rest of day. But also, it felt as if it was a gift he was giving himself, too; he was so engaged, alive, vibrating with life and discovery.

And he succeeded in erasing that last awful memory from her—or at least pushing it to the back of her mind where it belonged.

They built a sandcastle out of that luscious pink sand. Though she'd been afraid to get back into the sea, he coaxed her in, and they chased each other through the shallows, splashing.

"Do you think you know how to swim?" he asked her.

She searched through her mind. "I don't think so. I mean obviously, a few rudimentaries, enough to keep my head above water, but not enough to make a break for shore."

"Let's try teaching you."

This proved quite hopeless. Because of her near drowning she was afraid to get in too deep and she was terrified of getting her face wet, so he gave up after a while.

"But remember," he told her, "If my dad can learn to make cakes—and Mike—you can learn to swim. You can learn to do anything."

As night fell, the barbecue was fired up again,

and this time hamburgers were grilled, and then a fire was lit on the beach.

A guitar came out. And a harmonica.

She knew some of the tunes and some she did not. Everyone sang along. Even Gage.

"Your voice," she told him, "is as bad as mine."

"I know," he said, and sang louder.

And so, so did she.

It was so simple and so joyous, singing around the fire as the sparks rose up to meet the stars. She felt a part of something. It was, she was fairly certain, not a normal feeling for her. She was determined to enjoy every second of it while it lasted.

She also, as the evening unfolded, became aware she had been kidding herself about Gage being the kind of man you *could* fall in love with.

Because she was already more than halfway there. But in the back of her mind lurked another awareness, and that was of how quickly it all could change.

Gone in a blink.

Just like the fairy tale. *Poof.*

CHAPTER SIXTEEN

IT HAD BEEN such a super day. Gage tried to remember the last time he'd had so much fun.

Of course, after she'd had that last memory, he had wanted, somehow, to give Hailey the best day of her life. And by sharing some of his own memories, he'd been letting her know he understood, letting her know people could come through the rough stuff, and sometimes it made them *better.*

He felt that memory of her mother on the couch at her birthday party was part of who she was, but in a good way. It was what made her walk through the *Seas du Jour* and notice the people instead of the stuff. It was what made him want to show her, maybe, how things could be.

What he hadn't been expecting was how sharing confidences that were supposed to be for her benefit had made him feel.

Listened to.

Safe.

He didn't have a moment's anxiety that the most personal parts of his family's life would be turned into headlines. It wasn't just that he trusted Hailey.

It was *more*. He *loved* trusting her. He loved the intensity of the way she listened to him; he loved how compassion deepened the blue of her eyes and worked around the edges of her mouth.

He could feel himself leaning toward something she offered, as if she could chase away a loneliness he hadn't even been aware he was experiencing.

When they came back aboard the yacht, one of the crewmen told him Seth needed to see him and it was urgent.

Gage turned to Hailey. "I'll be back in a minute."

She was sun-kissed and sand-encrusted. Her hair was an absolute mess, and she was without a doubt the worst singer he had ever heard. And possibly the worst volleyball player, as well.

Gage had been around women who wore bathing suits without enough material in both pieces to make a hankie, who paraded their bodies boldly, who flaunted their certainty around their sexuality and the power it gave them.

Hailey was the antithesis of that. She had worn a one-piece that reminded him of something his mother might have chosen, and yet when he'd applied that sunscreen to her back, it had felt as if his world was blowing to smithereens—he had been so aware of the sensation of her skin under his fingertips.

The very fact she hinted, rather than shouted, about her body, made her unbelievably sexy. She had a sweet, shy self-consciousness about her, a total unawareness of her powerful allure—an allure that had deepened as they'd shared confidences.

It made him want to be the one who drew her sensuality out of her, showed her how to embrace and celebrate it. And at the same time he wanted to be that person, he felt guilty for wanting it, like a priest being tempted to break his vows, because that was her intriguing contradiction.

She was purity. And she was temptation.

She had a way of being in the world as if everything was brand-new. And, of course, because of the memory loss, maybe that was how it was to her.

But her enthusiasm, her delight in tiny things, her way of seeing the world, her verve for trying new experiences, made everything feel brand-new to him, as well.

"I'm going to go shower," she said.

The old him wanted to shower together. The old him wanted to move it to the next level and explore all of her, including her feminine mysteries, more deeply.

But the man she made him want to be, the new him, had to practice discipline. His world had always been full of discipline—working out, eating right, not partying—but doing what he felt was right *for her* was part of the brand-new him he was exploring. He left her and made his way through the yacht to Seth's office and opened the door.

"Hey, what's up?"

Then he noticed a worn suitcase and a small purse by Seth's desk.

"We found her," Seth said quietly.

Yes, they had. They had found her at sea. Today, Gage had had a sense of having really found her, but also of having found himself at the same time.

When she'd asked him to share his childhood, it had felt so safe. It was who he was *now* that he wasn't yet ready to reveal to her.

That sense of safety had deepened as he had started to talk to her, felt the way she listened, saw how eminently trustworthy she was.

So many of the things he'd confided in her about growing up he had never really said to anyone. Was it her own unhappy childhood that had made him want to show her parts of his that he rarely thought about? In speaking of those mostly disowned portions of his life, he had realized what an integral part of him they were. Maybe even the most important parts of him were in those things he didn't ever talk about.

But he had also become more and more comfortable with the feeling of being wholly himself—not just showing the strengths, not just the part that dazzled the world—to a world unaware, and probably uncaring, of the history that had made him who he was.

Seth gestured at the bags. "I mean we found out *who she is*."

Gage felt as if his heart was going to stop. What if everything he had come to believe was not true? What if, despite all evidence to the contrary, she was married? What if she had a whole life that was waiting for her back home?

One that would never include him.

"Her name is Hailey Witherspoon. She checked into a vacation rental. It was one of those contactless kinds—you know, where the landlord sends you a keypad code, and you let yourself in? She sent in the arrival survey, so he knew she'd gotten there. But he didn't give her another thought until she didn't respond to his checkout reminders four days later. Today."

Gage frowned.

"And then he went to his property and knocked on the door and there was no answer. So he called the number he had for her from outside the door and could hear it ringing inside. He felt the first little niggling of alarm, but he told himself she might be having a shower or a nap or maybe stepped out without her phone for a minute. So he left it an hour and then went back. When she still didn't answer, he used his master key to get in. It was apparent to him she hadn't been there since that first night. Her suitcase was on the bed, but it hadn't even been opened. Her phone was plugged in next to the bed, filled with notifications. So, he called the police, and they put two and two together and called me. Her things were delivered an hour ago. I didn't touch anything. I figure that's for her to do, now."

"I'll take it to her," Gage said.

He felt a heaviness that had nothing to do with

her lightweight luggage as he picked it up and made his way to her room.

Somehow, the whole day had felt like it promised new beginnings, a new way of being in the world that was more complete, that was stripped bare of all the distractions, that held out the promise of living more honestly and fully, of sharing his experiences, his whole self with another human being.

But the suitcase in his hand felt as if it might be an ending.

He knocked.

"Come in."

He opened the door. She had not showered yet, and was still in her bathing suit. One strap was falling down off her shoulder.

She looked up at him, her sun-kissed face shining with radiance.

But then she frowned and got up. "Gage? What is it?"

She saw the luggage and went very still. She lifted her eyes back to his.

"A vacation rental called the police this morning when you failed to answer checkout notices." He handed her the purse.

She staggered backward and sat on the edge of the bed. She opened it slowly, pulled out a wallet and then took a deep breath. She found what looked to be a driver's license.

"Hailey Witherspoon," she said, a bit dazed. She glanced at the license again. She read out an address, and then her birth date. "I'll be twenty-seven in three weeks," she said.

He had the most awful thought of her sitting alone with a cupcake.

She looked pale and distressed.

"Do you want me to leave you? To sort through your things? To see if they trigger any memories?"

"I want you to stay. I'm kind of scared."

He sank down on the bed beside her as she looked into the purse.

The first thing she brought out was her phone. She stared at it without recognition, but then she tapped in a code.

"I remember that," she said.

"That makes sense. That's the number every single person uses dozens of times every day."

"There's a notice," she said, and tentatively tapped it. "It's an itinerary. It says I'm flying from Chania to Athens tomorrow and then going on to London."

It felt as if a fist squeezed at his heart. He wasn't ready to let her go. It felt as if he had just found her. And yet, there was a sense of being on a train now that was going in only one direction, that could not be stopped.

"You don't have to act as if that's carved in stone. You can change your plans. You can stay here as long as you want," he said.

Hailey scowled and he looked over her shoulder to see at what. She had missed calls and texts.

She sounded the names out loud, like a child just learning to read.

"Gregory Hamilton," she said. "Bethany Wilson."

"Do they mean anything to you?"

"Bethany," she said slowly. "She's the friend who gave me the necklace."

"Gregory?"

She shook her head. She poked at the screen. A man's picture came up. She gasped audibly and pressed her fingers to her temples.

Gage stared at the photo, like a warrior catching the first sight of his opponent. Had this man tossed Hailey into the sea? Could he be responsible for what happened next if this man had deliberately tried to harm Hailey?

A little whimper of pure pain escaped her.

"Hey, maybe that's enough for now," Gage said soothingly.

But she wouldn't stop. "It feels as if I'm right on the edge of something."

"Well," he said uneasily, "that could be a cliff."

And still she apparently felt compelled to peer at her phone.

He could see the dread on her face, and he could feel his own heart starting to thud with alarm.

"Hailey," he said. "Don't."

But then she read a message out loud.

Begging your forgiveness. Please be a part of our day.

Her face went white. She started to breathe very heavily.

"Hey," Gage said more firmly, "that's enough for now."

He tried to take her phone from her, but she turned quickly, blocking his effort.

She scrolled quickly to the messages from the other frequent caller. "My friend, Bethany," she said, her voice hoarse, touching the hollow of her throat.

"I think you need to stop for now."

"I can't," she whispered. She closed her eyes. She looked like someone in a film, remembering something with the help of hypnosis.

"I'm at Bethany's flat," she said, her voice dull and robotic. He felt terrified by that voice.

"We live in the same neighborhood. I think I teach nursery school. Maybe we even teach at the same school. All three of us."

"I don't know if this is a good idea," Gage said slowly. "Maybe you should wait. I'll call the doctor."

But it was like she had taken her finger out of a dam; the flow had started and she couldn't stop it.

"It's the last day of school. We're finished. Summer break is starting.

"We always go in and out of each other's houses. I go into hers and I call her name, but she doesn't answer. I just think she's not home yet, but then I hear giggling. I can't wait to find out what's so funny."

When he realizes he can't make her stop, Gage takes her hand. And squeezes.

Hailey's heart was beating so hard she felt like it might pound out of her chest.

She remembered now. She'd followed the sound of her friend's happiness to her bedroom door. There was no reason to think anything was going on. It was the middle of the day. She and Bethany had always gone in and out of each other's houses, as if they were sisters.

At first her mind couldn't even grasp what she was seeing. Bethany was in bed. Not alone.

Hailey turned to run, mortified at her error, when something stopped her.

The slender sweep of his back? The way his neatly cut blond hair touched the back of his neck?

It was Gregory.

Hailey's fiancé.

In bed with her best friend.

"Bethany and Gregory," she whispered out loud. "I found them together. My best friend and my fiancé."

She recalled with unfiltered clarity the stunned looks on both their faces.

And then she'd run and run and run.

No wonder she had remembered laughter and a feeling of connection followed by fury.

Gage's arms were around her, and he was stroking her hair. Her face was against his chest, and she could feel the steady beat of his strong heart, as her tears soaked through his shirt onto his chest.

"It's okay," he said, over and over. "It's okay."

He let her cry until she had no tears left. His shirt was soggy.

"I think I need to be by myself now," she finally whispered. After he left, she'd opened her sad-looking suitcase. The contents inside were in a jumble.

She picked up a crushed dress. She could feel the cheapness of the fabric. Underneath was underwear. The kind, as Eleni had pointed out, that a woman might wear to play sports.

Nothing was lovely. Everything was inexpensive. Most of it showed signs of wear as cheap clothing tended to do. T-shirts with loose necks, faded shorts, rubber sandals.

No wonder her fiancé had looked elsewhere. She deserved it. No wonder, from the first moment of feeling the pull of Gage, she had known how very dangerous attraction was.

What she did not deserve was this. Living in the lap of luxury in a gorgeous yacht with a gorgeous man who was about to find out what an imposter she was.

Today, she had *almost* felt as if she belonged. Almost. Now, she wondered if, while she'd been happily indulging in a completely unreal fantasy, her own mind had been protecting her from the truth by not letting her remember.

But hadn't the voice been there, all along, in the back of her mind?

Who do you think you are?

It felt as if the life she was remembering she'd had was crashing into the one she'd experienced for the last few days. The result was going to be cataclysmic, especially now that she had become aware just how easy it would be to fall in love with Gage.

Did she really think, if she couldn't hold the interest of a man like Gregory, she would be able to hold Gage's interest, long-term?

They were from totally different worlds. Her mother's drinking—and her meanness when she drank—had played the soundtrack behind Hailey's entire life.

She thought of what Gage had told her about his experiences growing up. Oh, yes, there had been challenges and terrible moments.

But they had conquered them as a family. Being a family had allowed them to find the strength to deal with whatever life threw at them.

Love had given them the tools not to stay stuck in their misery the way her mother had been stuck.

No doubt there had been cookies and milk after school. And Christmases where the children felt a sense of excitement instead of a sense of dread.

What had she had after school? A flat with dirty dishes in the sink and a mother not there, though the smell of her cigarette smoke was always hanging in the air.

Christmas had been about not enough money, *more* drinking, *more* uncertainty.

Hailey recalled the refuge of school. That's why

she'd been drawn to children. She had struggled and scrabbled to make her dream come true. She was the first in generations of her family to go to college and get a postsecondary education.

Had her mother been proud of her?

No, she'd been too busy blowing out cigarette smoke, looking at her with slitted eyes.

Who do you think you are? Better than the rest of us?

She'd left the tawdry, chaotic world of her mother behind to the best of her ability. She taught nursery school. It was a world of sanctuary and order, but sometimes, still, her mother inserted herself into that.

Making Hailey's commitment to children—especially the Billies of her world—even more important to her. Somehow, she had become determined to give those children everything she'd not had.

Love. Acceptance. Safety.

She loved them and built them up and gave them a safe place, the same as school had given to her.

And then she had met Gregory, and it had seemed as if she was going to get what she had always, always longed for.

A *normal life*.

He had seemed so bloody attractive, not because of his looks, but because he'd held out a golden ring that seemed to promise her stability, tradition, security. Was it all a lie, a fantasy she had talked herself into believing, just like the last few days had been?

She threw herself down on the bed and sobbed her heart out.

And then she realized that the awful discovery of Bethany and Gregory in bed together wasn't even recent. It had happened last summer, a year ago. That's when she had taken Bethany's necklace off. He'd said he didn't want the ring back.

Like he thought she would want it? A souvenir, perhaps, of their time together?

She had transferred to a different school. She had convinced herself she was over it. She had devoted herself to the children she looked after; she had poured all the love in her heart into them and only them.

It had felt as if she would survive. That she would never trust again, but her kids would be enough for her to have a rich, wonder-filled life.

The event that had happened recently, Hailey remembered now, was the arrival of their wedding invitation.

With a note inside it, signed by both of them.

We love you so much. We cannot imagine our day without you.

That's when she had cut her hair, wanting to look every bit as ugly and as unworthy as she felt. Gregory had loved her thick, lustrous hair. With every lock snipped, she had thought, *take that*, as if she was getting back at him, not herself.

Then, her new haircut complete, she had booked a holiday to anywhere that was available.

That's how she had come to be standing at the edge of the harbor, just shortly after she'd arrived in Chania that evening. She'd left her luggage in her apartment. Her phone had been nearly dead so she had plugged it in. Already, there were messages from both of them that she didn't want to read.

Exhausted, heartbroken, she had opened her small jewelry box. In it was the Best Friends Forever pendant she had worn around her neck since she was twelve. She had attached the engagement ring to the same chain.

She'd thrown it as far as she could, but it seemed she couldn't even get that right, because it had still fallen short of the sea.

And so she'd climbed over a wall, and onto slippery rocks, determined to dispose of that damned necklace and ring.

But somehow, flinging it with all her might, she had lost her balance on the slippery rocks. And her world had gone blank until she found herself struggling in the water

She closed her eyes, welcoming the blackness that came this time.

A soft knock on the door woke her. It was full dark now. She felt disoriented at first. But then it all came back to her.

She knew exactly who she was.

And that was nothing. And nobody. She had allowed herself to feel a sense of belonging on this ship; she had allowed herself to feel connections with other people. She would have never allowed those things if she'd had any memory of the past. Now, she was convinced every single thing she'd felt over the last few days was fake.

"Yes?" she asked. She sat up on the bed.

The door opened. Hailey was thankful for the darkness in the room, because she knew her face would be blotchy from crying.

"I've been asked to deliver this," Brody said. "And an invitation. Gage wondered if you would like to dine on deck with him tonight? In an hour?"

He set a rectangular box inside her door, a square of white envelope on top of it.

She knew, in light of all she had discovered, the obvious answer was no. This was not her world, and never would be. She had a ticket to leave here tomorrow and she had to take it.

But, still, she could not resist going over and retrieving the parcel and the card. She opened it with trembling hands.

It was the silver-gray dress she had tried on in the store. She didn't know how he had made that happen, but she unfolded the tissue paper from around it and took it out of the box. She pressed it to her face and felt the silky promise it had shown her.

Who she could be.

Of course, it wasn't true. She'd be like a child playing dress-up.

On the other hand, she was being offered one more night.

Not just in this glorious world.

But with *him*.

One more night with Gage before she had to give it all up and go back to her real life.

She shook out the dress and remembered exactly how she had looked in it. How she had felt. Could she really say no to that? To having one more memory to hug to herself? One more small glimpse inside the fairy tale before—as she had always known—*poof*, it was over?

An hour later, Hailey stared at herself.

She had managed to erase the worse damage from the crying with cold water compresses and makeup. Her eyes, with the help of just a touch of mascara and shadow, looked like sparkling jewels; her cheekbones looked even higher and more sun-kissed with a hint of blush; the curve of her lips, outlined with a pearly pink gloss, looked full and sensual.

Even her cropped hair looked slickly sophisticated. Especially with the addition of the earrings, the cut looked intentional.

A woman sure enough of herself, of her femininity, of her sensuality, to cut her hair shorter than a boy.

But in her face, she also saw a new depth and sensitivity, a fledgling maturity. A woman who, yes, had had her heart broken.

And yet had refused to let it break her.

She didn't, in fact, feel fake at all.

Tonight, Hailey decided firmly, she would allow

herself to be a princess. Tonight, she would act as if it was all real.

And tomorrow, just like in the fairy tale, it would be over. And she would be on her way back to her own humble life.

But she would carry a new certainty in the strength of her own spirit that she'd not had before she'd been rescued from certain death, before she'd come aboard the *Seas du Jour*.

Before she had met Gage Payton.

CHAPTER SEVENTEEN

GAGE WAS NERVOUS as he stood at the railing on the main deck, looking out over the sea. It was a feeling that was generally foreign to him. He'd experienced it, sometimes, on the day of a big game, but then as soon as the game started, it was gone.

Still, just like in a big game, he wanted tonight to be perfect.

When he'd seen her heartbroken face—or maybe it had been that airline ticket, dated for tomorrow—Gage had known he wanted to erase every pain and heartbreak Hailey had ever felt.

And maybe convince her not to go—to stay here just a little while longer.

For her. Not for him. To protect her just a tiny bit longer, to give her a chance to recover some more. To let him show her that days like today didn't have to be the exception. They could be the rule. This was how good life could be.

From what Hailey had said, her wounds were still very fresh. It sounded as if her horrible betrayal was less than a week old. She was even more vulnerable now than she had been before she had remembered.

For the first time since the end of his football career, for the first time since Babba's betrayal, he *wanted* what he had felt on the beach today. He wanted to feel that bond with another person. But, at the same time, he knew he had to be very careful.

He wanted *her.*

He wanted her in every way it was possible for a man to want a woman.

But Hailey was not a Bouncy Brigade kind of woman. It required more of him, consideration of the fact that now would not be the time in her life where good decisions came from. And when she looked back at this decision, he wanted Hailey to consider it the best of her life.

So, tonight was his gift to her. A pure gift, the kind with no strings attached.

He wasn't a formal kind of guy, but he knew the dress he'd sent to her required more of him than shorts and a T-shirt. He had a tux on board, left over from when one of his close football buddies had gotten married here on the *Seas du Jour.*

He'd had the main deck prepared. There had been a faint unspoken excitement in the air, as the crew contemplated *romance.*

He didn't care if they wanted to muddy his altruism with such thoughts. It had made them do an exceptional job. The boundaries between the salon and the deck had been erased, the glass doors folded completely open.

The pool loungers had been stored, leaving an expanse of open space around the pool that candles and flower petals floated in. Soft music was being piped in on a stereo system so sophisticated it might have been live musicians.

At the railing, beside him, a table had been set up with white linens and candles as well as the exquisite place settings and wine glasses and cutlery that the yacht had come equipped with, but except for special occasions, like that wedding, were rarely used.

Gage caught a movement out of the corner of his eye and turned his full attention to the main entrance to the salon.

His breath caught in his throat as he saw Hailey step through it. He thought he had remembered the pure power of that dress, but now he realized he had not.

It looked as if she wore moonlight, the filmy dress clinging in all the right places, making her seem, not like a waif rescued, but rather like a goddess risen.

She looked exquisite and gorgeous…a film star ready for the red carpet, a model ready for the runway, *a princess ready for the ball.*

She hadn't seen him yet, and she paused, wide-eyed and deer-like both in her grace and the fact she looked as if she might bolt.

She took, finally, a hesitant step forward, and he came out of the shadows. Her gaze rested on him, and she smiled tentatively.

Still, it looked as if one false move and she would run, and so he stopped, knowing the decision whether to stay or go had to be hers. He was not aware he had been holding his breath until she stepped toward him instead of away.

He went to meet her.

He didn't say anything, at first, just took her hands and laid his forehead against hers.

"You look amazing," she told him.

"So do you," he murmured, then stepped back from her, but held her hands and let his eyes sweep over her.

"Marco," she whispered.

"Polo," he whispered back. "I hope the damned cat doesn't think we're calling him."

Somehow, he had said the right thing to break the ice, because she laughed.

"It's not romantic," he said. "I don't want you to get the wrong idea. What happened to you is pretty fresh. I'm just trying to make you feel a little better."

She stepped back from him. Her eyes were huge and beautiful and soft. She touched a finger to his lips.

"After you left, I remembered that finding them together was a whole year ago now."

He felt his heart begin to throb. His motives and his honorable intentions felt immediately muddy.

Suddenly he was the one who didn't know whether to bolt or whether to stay The door had suddenly burst open to moving forward with Hailey. And yet moving forward with this kind of woman required commitment. Honor. She didn't even know the full truth about who he was.

He chose to stay. He took her elbow, guided her to the table, pulled out the chair for her and then moved the one across from her to beside her instead. He threaded his fingers through her hand.

"Tell me."

"I guess I kept hoping it wasn't going to work out for them," she said softly. "Not that I wanted either of them back in my life, but I wanted somehow for them to get their comeuppance. I wanted it not to work. I wanted for that part at least to be true. That it had just happened between them, that it was a mistake, that they saw the price—the loss of friendships—was too much and that the flimsy chemical attraction they had couldn't hold a relationship together."

She grimaced. "But, oh no. Almost on the anniversary of it happening—when I'd just started summer break—I went to the letter box and found one of those heavy linen envelopes in it. An invitation to their wedding, if you can believe it. As if they had absolutely no understanding how deep their betrayal went. I went back into my place and bawled my eyes out and cut my hair."

"Why did you cut your hair?" he asked softly.

"Because it seemed like a fast way to leave the old me behind—a woman who could fall for a man like that—and become something new. Because it was one of my best features, and I didn't want men like Gregory to find me attractive anymore. Ever again. Maybe even because I wanted people to be able to tell, at a glance, I was *damaged.* And then I booked a trip to the first place that was available and in my price range, so that I wouldn't be anywhere near London on their wedding day, and so that I could try on being a new person."

Slowly, her voice halting, Hailey told him about finding herself at the water's edge, her determination to get rid of any reminders of *them*, slipping, falling, finding herself in the sea.

Gage was listening to her. Of course he was. Every word felt like a blow. It hurt how deeply she saw herself as damaged, how she had cut off her hair as a warning flag to the world. When he thought of her fiancé, he was a nine-year-old boy again, with L-O-V-E written on his knuckles, only this time he would make the connection.

But at war with his compassion for her was a fanning to life of celebration. There was no denying that inside him a voice was singing, *It's been a year, it's been a year, it's been a year.*

He touched her cheek. It felt as if fireworks were going off in his brain. It wasn't recent. Her heartbreak was real, but not fresh. She had come here for closure.

Or maybe something even bigger—a meeting with fate, though a few days ago, Gage would have probably scoffed at such things.

He scanned her face, looking for any sign that she recognized him now her memory had returned.

There was none. He knew it was time to come clean, and yet he wanted to ride this wave—of her being attracted to him just for himself—for a little while longer.

Was she as attracted to him as he was to her? He was pretty sure she was, and there was one way to find out for certain.

"What an amazing number of twists and turns it took," he said.

"Twists and turns?"

"For destiny to bring you to me."

And then he did what he had been wanting to do forever. Waiting to do forever. He committed.

He kissed her.

And she kissed him back, which answered his question, completely, about reciprocal attraction. Hailey met his lips with wonder and with welcome and with a raw hunger that took him by surprise, even as he embraced it.

"The beard," she whispered.

He knew he would shave it off in a second if she didn't like it.

"It's wonderful. The texture. It adds a layer of something…"

What he wanted to do, right then and there, was gather her in his arms, pick her up, carry her to his stateroom and love her as she had never been loved before, with *layers* she had never expected.

But, he also wanted to be *more* than that man.

"You know how I told you it wasn't romantic?"

he whispered to her and could hear the hoarseness of desire in his own voice.

She nodded.

"It's romantic, now," he told her, and he made sure that it was. He reached for the bottle of champagne, uncorked it, poured some in each of their flutes.

He raised his glass to her. She raised hers to him. They touched the rims and sipped. All he could think was that her lips had tasted so much sweeter than the wine.

A black-jacketed waiter came out with shrimp and avocado towers as appetizers. This was followed by whole lobsters.

"I don't know how to eat this," she whispered, as if someone was watching.

"Thank goodness for that," he replied, and broke the lobster shell, tore a tender morsel of meat from the claw, dipped it in butter and popped it in her mouth. Her eyes widened as she chewed.

"Gage. That is the most amazing thing I have ever tasted. I mean besides..." Her eyes wandered to his lips, and she laughed softly and blushed sweetly.

He broke off another piece, but this time she took it from his fingers and held it to his lips. He nibbled her buttery fingers after.

Morsel by exquisite morsel they fed each other, their awareness of each other sparking in the air between them like a broken power line snapping on the ground.

Wine.

Dessert.

Electricity crackling in the air.

"I don't come from this. I've remembered everything—" she said, and then with a hint of wry self-deprecation "—unfortunately."

"I don't come from this, either," he said quietly.

"But you come from a normal family."

"What's that mean?"

"Mother, father, sister, nieces, nephews."

She sounded heartbreakingly wistful.

"A Christmas tree," she guessed. "Family dinners, board games."

"You didn't have a Christmas tree?" he asked.

"Once," she said. "My mother dragged one home on Christmas Eve. Who knows if it was given to her or she simply took it?"

"Hailey…"

"No," she said, and touched his lips with her fingertips. "Never mind. It's not for tonight. At least not until after midnight."

As if on cue, the music changed from background sound to something else.

She cocked her head. "Is this—"

"It's the soundtrack," he told her, "from *Beauty and the Beast*."

He held out his hand to her, and they rose from the table. They danced on the deck around the pool, where the lounge chairs had been cleared.

He could see the pure joy in her as she unleashed her full sensuality in that dance. They danced and laughed until they were breathless with it and so aware of each other that it bordered on painful.

And then the tempo of the music suddenly slowed.

She stared at him. Her eyes sparkled with tears as the music cascaded over the deck and out across the water. She came against him, her head resting on his heart, his hand on the small of her back, pressing her closer, feeling as if he could never have her close enough. They swayed beneath the stars to "a tale as old as time and a song as old as rhyme."

Gage's efforts to be *more* than that man collapsed. He surrendered to the "*old as time*" part of the man-woman dance.

He picked her up and strode through the quiet vessel to his stateroom. He nudged open the door and carried Hailey through to his bed.

She lay on it, wide-eyed and beautiful, a goddess in that dress.

She opened her arms and he fell into them. It felt as if it was a moment destined since his arms had first closed around her in the darkness of the sea.

CHAPTER EIGHTEEN

GAGE PAYTON HAD known the pure exhilaration of triumph more often than most men. He had run winning touchdowns that had snatched victory from the jaws of defeat.

He had stood on mountain peaks that his strength and grit, discipline and determination, had allowed him to conquer.

He had parlayed his company, Touchdown, into one of the most successful businesses in the world.

And yet he had never felt a moment, not in his entire life, like the one where he had swum out to Hailey, reached her and felt her arms curl desperately around his neck.

From the instant those huge blue eyes, framed in thick lashes crusted with droplets of water, had fastened on him, and he had seen the hope flicker to life in them.

And felt it flicker to life within himself.

In that moment, in the sea, it seemed as if all the hours of physical training for his entire life had not been to propel him to the glory of wins on the football field, but had been to prepare him, instead, for the moment when her arms had closed around him out in that dark ocean.

Now, as Hailey lay down on the bed, her arms open to him once more, Gage felt a surge of absolute certainty such as he had never felt in his life before.

He had been born for this.

He had been born to answer the call of that precise moment in time that had led him and Hailey unerringly to each other.

For months he'd been struggling with the sense of *something missing*. It had been nebulous, but now it was crystal clear to him. He had longed for what all men long for. Passion. Love. Connection. Family. Home. He had longed for those things and denied the strength of his longing because he had thought, after the betrayals he'd suffered, that the price of his success and his fame was that he could not have what ordinary men took for granted.

Looking at Hailey, in that dress woven from moonlight, her eyes holding the ancient secrets that existed between a man and a woman, a voice spoke to him with quiet certainty.

She's it. She's the something that has been missing.

There was no other ending more perfect for this perfect night, Hailey thought, than to find herself in Gage's bed. He flung himself down into her outstretched arms, and she felt the beautiful crush of his body against hers.

He held most of his weight off her, taking it with his elbows, gazing down at her with wonder.

He ran his hands over her hair and touched it with his lips, anointing it, and then her forehead and then each of her eyes, the tip of her nose and finally, the bow of her mouth.

But when she tried to pull him closer, to greedily take more of what his mouth offered, he held her back and then slid down the length of her.

Gage kissed her toes and then began at the hem of her dress, moving it up one tiny increment at a time, torturing her with the exquisite slowness of his unveiling, allowing his lips to caress and torment each part of her he revealed. He kissed her calves, her knees, her inner thighs, alternating between fire and rain.

He slid the dress upward, kissed the waistband of her panties, then her belly button, and then the lacy fringe of her bra.

He nudged her arms up and slid the dress over her head, tossed it away and regarded her underwear-clad body with raw hunger, made even sexier by how well he leashed it.

He reached behind her back, and with a flick, freed the clasp on her bra. He brushed it away and drank in what he had revealed. Being looked at by him, being naked before him, felt as natural, as right, as inevitable, as moonlight being dissolved by the coming of day.

Without taking his eyes from her eyes, his fingers, trembling ever so slightly with the effort of keeping his desire under control, tugged at the waistband of her panties, and he moved them down her legs. Hailey wiggled to get them off, found them with her toe, and they joined the dress on the floor.

He moved, straddling her, up on his knees, shrugging off the suit jacket and then the tie. She licked her lips and felt the dryness of her mouth as he dispensed with his buttons of his dress shirt, one by one, and then peeled it away, revealing the broad, golden surface of his chest to her.

The shirt dispensed with, he settled his weight back on top of her, and she felt skin on skin, a sensation more intoxicating than the champagne she had drunk tonight.

With impossible grace, he disengaged from her, stood for a moment at the side of the bed, and then, smiling slightly at her eyes on him, stripped off the remainder of his clothing.

And then he was beside her, again, tracing every line of her with a fingertip, his touch featherlight and reverent.

His exploration felt exquisitely right and breathtakingly beautiful.

He mapped her body, first with his fingers, then his hands and then his lips. It was as if he had come upon a fire, nearly out, and was using his breath to breathe the sparks back into being, then fanning the fire he'd coaxed to life. The heat built and built and built into an inferno that threatened to turn them both to ash.

And just as she thought it would incinerate them, Gage backed off, teasing her, letting things cool, tenderly tormenting, trailing hints of that fire over her eyelids, her throat, her breasts, her midriff, her belly button, the sweet softness between her legs.

He whispered endearments in her ear, and then his tongue chased the words.

Her whole body was vibrating, alive in ways she had not known it was possible to be alive.

Perhaps in ways she would have missed, had life been obedient and followed her plan for it.

No mere mortal plan, either. What was unfolding between them defied planning, taming, defining, capturing.

This was primal, magnificent energy—the life force itself—let loose, unchained, untamed.

It was both fire and rain.

It was scorching sunlight and cool moonlight.

It was tenderness and it was fury.

It was storm and it was calm.

All of those things, melding together, until there were no boundaries between any element of earth and heaven, until they swirled in tighter and tighter circles of ferocious magnificence, faster and faster, until they fused into one, until they became each other, until that final fiery explosion separated them again and broke them into a million fragments spewed into that space from which all creation had sprung in the first place.

For a moment, Hailey was suspended there, in that place of both separation and connection, and then she fell back into her body, felt Gage sigh against her, roll from her, gather her to him, before both of them gave into oblivion, into the exhaustion of utter fulfillment.

They slept in the circle of each other's arms.

When Hailey woke up, she was not sure if minutes had passed or hours. *Seas du Jour* was rocking gently, a mother rocking the cradle of her children.

Gage was on his stomach, his arm still thrown across her, something deliciously possessive about the drape of that strong limb across her belly. She turned her head, ever so slightly, so she could look at him.

His head was turned toward her and the moon bathed the planes of his face, his complexion even more golden after being in the sun today. She took in the beautiful curls, the long lashes, the straight nose, the fullness of those beard-framed lips. She was certain that if she could taste them every second of every day for the rest of her life it would forever feel as if she hadn't had enough. She drank in the line of his back, the tangle of his hair; she relished how beautiful he was and what had just happened between them.

She closed her eyes again but sleep would not come. Their lovemaking had filled her with a thrumming energy.

She opened her eyes again, let them adjust to the darkness. A kind of puzzlement began to push at the edges of her bliss.

What exact position did Gage have on *Seas du*

Jour that he had brought her to the master suite, the space that had not been on their tour this morning?

Impossibly, it was even better than hers. This suite was obviously the most luxurious on the vessel. It was far bigger, more glamorous than hers was, every single thing about it whispering—not shouting—success, arrival, unfathomable wealth.

Hadn't the whole Cinderella evening—the dinner and the dancing, the service from the staff, the respect for privacy—had the same aura that was present in this room shimmering around it?

And what role did he have on this ship that allowed for that?

She realized that all this time, it had been a given that they didn't know who she was.

But with a faint feeling of panic rising in her, Hailey realized she didn't really know who *Gage* was either.

Did Gage use this luxurious accommodation whenever the owner wasn't on board? With or without his permission?

But that premise did not ring true to Hailey. Somehow, she did not get the impression he was a man to take what wasn't his.

And yet, who was she to trust her impressions? She remembered, now, that Gregory had never seemed like anything but an earnest, geeky, sweet teacher, just like herself. He hadn't seemed like a man who would ever take what wasn't his or break a rule either.

And yet he had taken her best friend.

Broken the biggest taboo of all.

And that Bethany, her childhood best friend, could have been a willing participant in such a taboo had shaken Hailey's whole sense of the world.

Suddenly, that feeling of not knowing who people really were was overwhelming to her. It was why the danger sign had been flashing on and off in her brain ever since she'd met him. Had she ignored it at her peril?

But then, she realized, she had something she had not had even six hours ago.

And she didn't mean a man's scent on her skin.

She had her phone.

And for some reason she had tucked it into her purse tonight before answering Gage's invitation to join him.

She slipped from the bed, the night air cool, doing her best to ignore the sense of being alive that shimmered along her naked skin.

She took out her phone and slipped into the bathroom that adjoined his suite. She flicked on a light.

By now she should be accustomed to the opulence of the *Seas du Jour* but she was not. The bathroom had a tub big enough for two people at one end of it, looking out over a huge window to the sea. She was no expert on stone, but even to her, it looked like marble.

It was obvious this was his space. Discarded on the floor were the shirt and shorts he had worn earlier today.

Then she saw the glassed-in shower area, and

couldn't help but smile, despite a growing sense of unease. The sexy space—two shower heads, obviously designed for two people accustomed to showering together—had been turned into a cattery for Marco Polo. It was scattered with his toys and dishes. His litter box was in there.

As if she was not feeling besotted enough with Gage, she saw he had braided climbing ropes for the kitten out of towels. There was an adorable structure at one end that looked like an igloo. One paw extended languidly out of the towel-constructed house.

Turning away from the kitten she spied one of those thick white bathrobes like you found at very expensive hotels hanging by the shower.

It was obviously his. It was way too big for her, but she put it on anyway. The scent that clung to it made her want to just go back, shuck it off, slide into bed with him and let him take her places she had never been.

Where you had no questions.

Where you had no past.

But, she told herself sternly, no future either.

She forced herself to sit down. She was not sure she had ever been in a bathroom with a seating area in it before—a beautiful soft, buttery leather bench.

She opened her screen on her phone. She found her way to the internet. And she tapped in the name Gage Payton.

And watched, stunned, at what came up.

Gage in a football uniform. Gage holding trophies high. Gage, CEO, of a company. This company. Touchdown, the one he had told her owned the vessel.

There were literally hundreds of images with his name under them, and each one made it quite clear—as if *Seas du Jour* itself hadn't been enough—that he was quickly becoming one of the richest people in the world.

But even more distressing than the wealth—which so clearly put him out of Hailey's league—were the photos of him with women.

As she flicked through her phone, there were endless photos of him with gorgeous, sophisticated, famous, wealthy women. Women with perfect hair and makeup, with smoking hot bodies and priceless wardrobes.

Every single insecurity she had ever felt flooded her. What on earth had he ever found attractive about her? Was it only their forced proximity that had made him take her to bed? Or, worse, after her confiding in him, had he felt sorry for her?

She was struck by an overwhelming sense of who she really was.

Hailey, swiping once more through some of those pictures, knew she did not fit into his world and never, ever would.

She was and always had been the geeky girl, the bookworm. The kid in the wrong clothes with the bad haircut. The one who'd secretly longed to sit at the cool kids' table, even as she pretended to scorn them.

Dawn was slipping in the window when she stood up, wrapped the white robe tight around her, opened the door and went back into the bedroom. She wasn't putting that dress back on. She had to get from this room to hers before the ship was fully awake. She didn't want to be seen by the crew in what was obviously his bathrobe.

They would know.

She felt the blush of pure humiliation stain her cheeks.

Her hand was on the doorknob.

"Hey—" his sleepy voice stopped her "—where are you going?"

She turned and looked at him. She had to steel herself against the sight of Gage Payton waking up. She had to remind herself of those gorgeous actresses she had seen him with. How many of them had woken up beside him?

"I'm going home," she said tightly. "I have a flight to catch."

He hopped out of the bed, glanced down at himself without a trace of self-consciousness, but then dragged the sheet off the bed, wrapped it around his waist and came to her. He touched her chin and gazed down at her, with that charming, lopsided grin.

"Stay," he said.

Instead, she slipped her phone out of her pocket, opened it, held out the screen to him. He looked at it, his brow furrowed, and then he understood.

"Oh, that," he said, as if it was nothing.

CHAPTER NINETEEN

GAGE LOOKED DOWN at Hailey. He steeled himself against how she looked wrapped up in his too-big robe, but he knew when a woman was looking for something to be angry about and she definitely fell into that category.

"Oh, *that*," she said furiously. "When were you going to tell me? That you own this ship and a good portion of the world?"

He cocked his head at her, determined not to let her see how her obvious lack of trust in him was wounding him, especially after what they had shared last night.

"Most women wouldn't be getting their undies in a twist over discovering a man was *more* successful than they might have imagined," he said, managing to infuriate her further by keeping his voice very mild.

"You think I care about that?" she said, with more hiss than that kitten. "You think I care how successful you are? You *lied* to me."

"I didn't actually lie," he corrected her, even

though he knew it was a mistake. "I just didn't tell you everything."

"Like Gregory and Bethany didn't tell me everything?"

He did not let the shock of being compared to that despicable pair show on his face at all. He certainly wasn't going to lay himself bare at her feet right now, admitting that he'd wanted to be known for himself, just for once. And he wasn't going to justify himself by telling her about Babba's betrayal. That would only increase the unfamiliar feeling of vulnerability that was sweeping through him, knocking him off-balance.

"I'm leaving," she said.

"How are you going to do that?" he needled her.

"Swim if I have to!"

"That went well for you last time," he reminded her.

"I'll find a way."

"Good," he said, and only when he saw the flash of hurt in her eyes did he realize he shouldn't have retaliated from a place of his own hurt feelings.

"How dare you let me think I could compete with the likes of these women? You've been with a princess, for heaven's sake!"

There was his name linked, *again*, with the most famous of the Bouncy Brigade! It made him feel anew the frustration of living his whole adult life in the spotlight.

If she didn't look so angry—so unwilling to trust him, so happy to jump to conclusions, exactly the same as everyone else when he'd thought she was different—he could have set her straight. He would have laid that insecurity to rest for her. Told her that nobody he had ever seen in the past could hold a candle to her.

But he wasn't going to beg her to trust him. Given all that had passed between them in the last few days, Hailey's whole attitude was unbelievably insulting. He'd been 100 percent convinced they had a connection. He had trusted her with things about himself he had never told anyone else. And even that wasn't enough for her.

Had it all been just a mirage? It cut him to the quick that a woman who he had revealed so much of himself to—not just with words, but with actions, too—could apparently find nothing about him that would make her want to stay.

Without another word, he turned his back on her, tucked his sheet tight around himself, went into the bathroom and shut the door. He let the sheet drop, planning to shower. The damn cat was in there, though! Still, he stayed in there, giving her time for her temper to subside, for her to reason things out. He might have even pictured her sitting on the bed, waiting to apologize to him.

A fantasy, of course, because he quickly heard the stateroom door slam, and when he went back into the bedroom, all that was left of her was that puddle of a dress on his bedroom floor and something that looked suspiciously like a glass slipper poking out from under his bed.

Still, he might have held out hope that she was going to return until the very second he heard a helicopter warming up and knew she wasn't coming back. Seth was the only other one on board with the authority to dispatch the helicopter. She must have gone to him. What had he expected his friend to do? Keep her against her will?

Consult him? But Seth didn't know what had happened last night, which was a mercy, really. Given that they had discovered her identity, he had probably thought Hailey's request to leave the vessel—flight home already scheduled—had been reasonable and not worth waking his boss up for.

It took everything he had not to completely unman himself by running up there to the helicopter deck and begging her to stay.

And then, when the helicopter was gone, not taking that shoe out from under his bed and throwing it as far as he could into the ocean.

Which would be plenty far. He had one of the world's best throwing arms, after all. Ask anyone.

An hour later, he was in his office, staring furiously at the screen. He hadn't known it was possible to go *back* levels in Football 4000, but there it was.

Failure.

A soft knock came on the door. He was going to pretend he wasn't here, but it would be better to act as though nothing had happened.

"Yup?"

The door opened. He glanced over his shoulder.

Seth. He didn't want to look at Seth, who could read people better than anyone else he'd ever known.

"She's gone," Seth said from behind him. Was there something faintly accusing in that tone?

"Okay," he said.

"She left most of her stuff."

Thanks, I know, he thought. *Including a glass slipper.*

"Give it all to charity," he said.

The cab dropped Hailey off in front of a row of small, terraced houses, on a street as far from any palace—or luxury superyacht—as you could possibly get.

She walked up to the front door and frowned to see that there was already a key in it. She tried the handle and found it unlocked. She took the key out of the door and slipped it in her pocket.

She stepped in and was assaulted by the smell of stale tobacco. At least she knew now who was there.

Her eyes adjusted to the dimness, and she saw her mother stretched out on the sofa, so reminiscent of her eighth birthday that Hailey felt slightly ill.

"Mum? What are you doing?"

Her mother shook herself awake, sat up, looked around, sank back against the sofa cushions and rubbed her temples.

"Oh," she said. "Look where I've ended up. Where've you been? What have you done to your hair?"

Her mother didn't even know where she'd been. Had she told her? Or had she given up long ago thinking she would have the kind of mother you shared your plans with, who might file a missing person's report if she didn't hear from you for a couple of days?

Hailey took in her mother's dress, a party dress, for sure, and ignored the question about her hair. "Maybe the question is where have *you* been?"

"At the wedding, of course!" Her mother tapped a cigarette out of her packet, lit it, inhaled with great pleasure. "Around the corner. That's why I ended up here."

Hailey remembered that, suddenly. They had booked a venue close to here, part of why she had absolutely *needed* to be away as Gregory and Bethany exchanged their vows. She'd had the awful thought, even though she absolutely would not go to the wedding, that she might still see them, run into the happy couple in her own neighborhood.

Last night, she realized. The evening wedding reception had been last night, just as she'd been lying in Gage's arms. No wonder it had never once crossed her mind. No wonder she had not played it out, scene by scene, in her mind.

Now she's walking down the aisle.

Now they're saying, I will.

Now they're exchanging rings.

"You went to Gregory and Bethany's wedding?" she asked, stunned. "But how could you?"

"I was invited," her mother said, lifting a shoulder her dress had fallen off from. She was so thin, the lifetime of neglect starting to take its toll on her. "I've known Bethany since she was twelve, for God's sake, Hailey."

As if, somehow, Hailey was in the wrong for questioning her mother going to the wedding and not her mother for acting as if this fickle behavior was okay.

"I can't believe you would go, knowing that they betrayed me."

A lift of that thin shoulder again. "Free booze," she said simply.

As if it was all that mattered.

And really, wasn't it all that had mattered to her mother as far back as Hailey's memories could stretch?

Suddenly she saw how all of it—her history with her mother—had really set her up for accepting so much less than she deserved.

For believing she wasn't ever good enough.

More, that she had to beg for love.

And that even as she begged for love, she would continue to give it unreservedly, set no boundaries, *enable* this kind of invasion of her space.

"You need to get out of my house," Hailey said, relieved she had pocketed the key when she came in.

Who would give someone like her mother a key to their house?

A very different person than the one she was now.

Her mother huffed, put out her cigarette with

deliberate slowness and then got up off the couch. She looked like she was considering asking about a shower or something to eat, but one look at Hailey's face stopped her.

"Oh, look," she jeered, "the mousy daughter finally becomes a warrior."

Somehow, Hailey knew that was true. All it had taken was a few days of feeling respected, worthwhile, cherished. It had changed everything. It had changed the way she saw herself.

You could never go back after that.

She knew she hadn't walked out on Gage just because he had lied to her. That was the flimsiest of excuses.

It wasn't his wealth and success she was afraid of. It wasn't really even the endless line of women she had found photos of him with.

Hailey didn't think a person could fake the experience Gage had given her on their final night together.

No, it was his family.

His dad made his mum birthday cakes. Gage dressed up for his niece for her birthday. Even the crew on board his ship embraced a family-like connection.

She had loved every minute of it.

And had waited to be called out as an imposter at the same time. Finding out who she really was had come as no surprise to her. But she had certainly wanted to flee before anyone else found out.

Her mother brushed by her. She actually looked for her key in the door.

"I can't see you again," Hailey said firmly. "I won't see you again, not as long as you're drinking."

"Get a little sun on your face, and you think you're all that," her mother taunted. "Your hair, by the way, looks awful."

Once, the sting of that would have been unbelievable.

Now, she looked at her mother, who had been lying on her couch, hung over, for nearly twenty-four hours. She was in no position to comment on anyone else's hair—hers was a rat's nest. She had makeup all over her face, and her dress was a wreck.

Hailey didn't feel any compulsion at all to engage with her or to hurt her back.

Instead, she started to laugh at the absurdity of it all.

Her mother shot her a wounded look and marched out the door.

Hailey set down her suitcase and looked around her tiny house. Especially with her mother's invasion being so obvious, it looked very small. It was a world away from what she had experienced aboard the *Seas du Jour*, of course.

On the other hand, even with her mother's presence clinging here like the smell of cigarette smoke, her tiny space was also a world away from what she had grown up with. In this humble home, she had created order and beauty.

There was a photo, framed, front and center on her coffee table. She had stripped the frame—an inexpensive charity shop find—down to its original wood, and there were test stripes on it in various stains and brown shades.

She picked up the photo and smiled. There they were. The class picture, *her* kids, twenty-two of them, one row on the ground and one on a bench, with her beaming as proudly as any mother beside them. She saw now, what she hadn't noticed before. Billy, her problem child, not looking at the camera, but instead looking at her. The love in those mischievous brown eyes was clear.

Hailey put the photo down. This was what she needed to remember: she had risen from the ashes of her childhood, and she had wrestled good from bad.

She was strong and she was resourceful.

Her betrayal by Bethany and Gregory had shaken her to the core. It had tried to drag her back into a childhood that had reinforced the message she was unworthy, that good things needed to be mistrusted. Their announcement of their wedding had further plunged her down that road of self-doubt and self-loathing.

But then she had done something different. She had picked up the phone and booked that trip and suddenly she could remember her motivation so clearly.

To get on with it.

To collect herself and pull herself up by her bootstraps.

To not count on other people to make her happy or to give her permission to live.

She had done something completely uncharacteristic by booking her trip to Greece. She had committed to saying goodbye to past pain and embracing whatever surprises and delights life might hold in the future.

Interesting that a vow for a new life would begin with a near death. Interesting and maybe symbolic.

Her time with Gage had been a rebirth, a glimpse of who she could be.

Oh, not fabulously wealthy, not surrounded by opulence and people waiting on her. She could sincerely say she couldn't care less about that.

No, Bethany and Gregory's betrayal had tried to snatch a belief in life from her.

And her few days with Gage had done the exact opposite. She wanted to be that person, fully engaged, fun-loving, on fire with excitement, open to the surprises, to the wonder that life held out every single day—a gift waiting to be opened.

She would not be who she had been after Bethany and Gregory had hurt her: defeated, ashamed, beaten-up, and worse, somehow believing she had *deserved* to feel like that.

Instead, she was committing, right here and right now to being the person Gage had seen, who she had been in his arms.

No, she had not left because he had lied to her.

She could actually see why a man like that would want to be seen for himself instead of his incredible wealth and accomplishments.

She had left because she carried the residue of unworthiness in her.

If she was ever going to find happiness—and love, true love—that's what had to be banished.

That sense of *I'll accept this because it's all I can expect. It's all I'm worth. I'll make all kinds of concessions and twist myself into a pretzel to make people love me.*

She saw suddenly what a blessing Bethany and Gregory's betrayal had been.

It, like nothing else, was the defeat that finally forced her to look not at them, but at herself. To find that thing inside herself that felt she deserved to be treated shoddily, that would put up with being treated as an afterthought in the name of love—and eradicate it.

The sense of being worthy couldn't come from Gage or from being spoiled on a boat like the *Seas du Jour*.

No, it had to come from within herself.

The work had to start now.

This was the difference Gage had created in her. She had no desire to retreat from life. In fact, she felt eager to engage with it, as if she had spent most of her life sleepwalking and was suddenly, wonderfully awake.

And eager to embrace *all* of it—the risks, the adventures, the inevitable catastrophes, falling in love, heartbreaks—all of it, part of an amazing dance that she had very nearly missed.

So that if love ever came calling again, she could step toward it, confident, worthy, ready, instead of walking away from it.

How to begin? She had the whole summer.

She opened her phone. What felt impossible?

She signed up for singing lessons. And then, she looked her fear of what had nearly happened to her in the ocean in the face.

It was time to learn more than how to keep her head above the water. Wasn't that really a metaphor for her life? It was time to learn to swim.

Gage was aware that he often annoyed his sister. He didn't remember ever making her truly angry. But she was angry now.

He'd let himself in the front door of her house after a brief knock. Had Kate's house always made him feel this?

It was all so normal: kids' backpacks at the door, a jumble of shoes, the couch cushions sliding off.

Longing.

His sister was sitting at the dining room table, blowing up balloons. She pinched one off when she saw him.

"What is that?" she said, glaring at the container in his hand.

No greeting?

"Where is everybody?" he asked, trying to buy a bit of time.

"They're still at the go-cart course. What is that?" she asked again, in a tone of voice that did not bode well for his birthday offering to Sam.

He looked down at the cat carrier, innocently, as if he was surprised to see it there. "Um, it's a pet carrier."

"I can clearly see that. What's in it?"

Marco Polo chose that moment to press his face into the front wire and hook a paw through the slats. He meowed piteously.

"Um…it's a kitten. I found him in Greece. Wandering the streets. Begging for scraps." A sharp memory of Hailey's face came with that recollection.

"Do not try that evasive charm on me, Gage. Answer the question."

"You haven't asked one," he pointed out reasonably.

"Why have you brought a kitten to Sam's birthday party?"

"Um—"

"You intended to give it to Sam as a gift! Don't even try to deny it."

"Look, you have to admit it's the best gift, ever. Uncle of the Year," he said, wagging his eyebrows and smiling at her, even though he'd already been warned his charms were useless on her.

"That is the worst idea you've ever had," she told him flatly.

Now did not seem like the time to remind her

of last year, when he'd brought a mini-motorcycle for his nephew and had been thwarted at the door.

"How could you swagger in here with that?" she asked him. "Bring it without asking me? What if the kids had been here?"

He thought *swagger* was an overstatement and unkind, but from the look on his sister's face, now might not be the time to argue it.

"Didn't you think the kids would get all excited and attached? And then I'm the bad guy when I say no?"

The container rocked in his hand as Marco Polo objected to his confinement and possibly the firm rejection of him.

The truth was, Gage hadn't thought of that. All he'd thought of was that he needed to get rid of the cat, as if he was the cause of his heartache, instead of just a reminder of it.

Still, he'd been unwilling to hand Marco Polo over to a stranger or a shelter, where he might never see him again, never know what happened.

A repeat of Hailey. Where he didn't know if he would see her again, despite his thoughts revolving around her every day. What was she doing? *How* was she doing?

"Pets are not gifts, Gage," Kate said, and he could see her anger reducing to a simmer, instead of a boil. "They require a commitment. A family in agreement."

"Do you think Mom and Dad would like him?" he asked hopefully.

She tilted her head and looked at him, *really* looked at him.

"It can't be easy to import a cat from Greece," she said.

"It's not." He winced at the memory of the hoops he'd had to jump through.

"I don't understand why you didn't find a good home for it there."

He didn't say anything.

Kate's mouth fell open. "You're *attached* to it," she said, astonished, as if he'd never been attached to anything in his life.

He lifted the cat container level with his eyes and poked a finger at Marco Polo, who immediately presented his chin for scratching.

"Marco Polo," he said, "the nine lives' rule is playing out in your adoption. This is the second rejection. Take heart, buddy, only seven more to go. You're really cute, so we might not need all of them."

His sister cocked her head. "Who did you try to give him to before?"

This was what you had to remember about Kate. She was terrifyingly intuitive. She was watching him very closely.

"Just somebody I spent some time with," he muttered. "She was actually with me when I found him."

"She?" Kate breathed.

As if he'd never had a woman in his life before! He glared at her.

"Why didn't she want him?"

He could have made up all kinds of stuff. He could have said she was allergic or lived in a place that didn't allow pets.

But suddenly he needed someone to know. The truth.

"She's not speaking to me," he said. "We parted on bad terms."

"You had a relationship?" Kate squealed.

"No." He thought of Hailey in his arms. "Well, not exactly. Maybe a chance at one. But I blew it."

"How?"

"I lied to her. She left."

"What did you lie about?"

"I didn't tell her who I was."

His sister was silent for way too long. "And when she found out who you were, she ran away from you? Instead of toward you?"

"As fast as she could."

"Why do you think that is?" she asked gently.

He suddenly knew *exactly* why it was. And it wasn't his lie. It was her insecurities.

After weeks of sulking and licking his wounds and contemplating how on earth that had happened to him, Gage now saw what he needed to do. He realized it wasn't about him at all. He wasn't sure if he could convince Hailey to give this a try, but he needed her to know something.

She *was* good enough.

She *was* worthy.

She was worth a thousand of any other woman he'd ever spent time with.

Then it occurred to Gage that he might be unworthy of Hailey! After all, his history with women wasn't ideal. But if she gave him a chance, could he prove, to both of them, that he was the man she needed? That she made him want to be a better man? His sister was smiling at him. How did she know these things? How did she know he had just had a rather earth-shattering epiphany?

"Gee," he said to Marco Polo. "Now I've got to figure out how to get you into England."

"An English girl," his sister said with a sigh, as if everything was already resolved. He remembered Kate had gone through a dreamy Brontë sisters phase.

"I'm not Rochester," he warned her darkly.

"Of course you aren't!" She seemed to think that was hilariously funny, as if he would be hopeless as a romantic lead, which was probably true.

But when she noticed the look on his face, she stopped laughing and said, "No mad wife locked in the attic."

"Huh," he said, and forgave her when she grinned at him. "Where do you want me to hide the cat so the kids don't see him?"

"Do," Hailey sang, happily following the note with a line from one of her favourite movies.

The teacher had asked her not to add that line

and to just sing the scales, but here at home, practicing, she couldn't resist.

"'"Re," she belted out, "a drop of Grecian sun."'"

A loud knock came on the door. The neighbors were not supportive of her singing classes. She glanced at the time.

It was already getting dark out at eight-fifteen at night. The shorter days were signaling that summer was coming to an end.

Despite her efforts to live fully—sightseeing in her home city, picnicking by herself, swimming and singing lessons—she was glad she'd soon be back at school.

She *needed* her kids. She needed their laughter and their affection.

The knock came again, stronger.

She went to the door and flung it open. There was a time when she would have meekly acquiesced to a neighbor's request to not make noise in her own home—despite one of them having a son in tuba lessons and the other side having screaming matches three times a week at all hours.

No one was there. Cowards, she thought. Then Hailey thought she heard a cat meowing, a faintly plaintive note to it.

Hadn't she just watched a crime documentary where a very evil person had put a tape recording of a crying baby outside a door to lure a woman out?

But she had spent so much of her life afraid, she just wasn't doing it anymore. Caution was good, of course, but too much caution killed joy.

"It's only just gone eight," she called to the unseen complainant. "I'll be wrapped up here in a few minutes."

She was considering giving up the singing lessons because she was not progressing as well as she had hoped. Singing did not give her the same sense of joy or accomplishment that she was experiencing with her swimming lessons.

On the other hand, she had, in absolute moments of weakness, done a bit of looking up around Gage.

There was a lot to see.

But one thing she had found out about him: he did not give up. She had made herself learn about football, and that was what she saw about him above anything else, as she went through old footage of his professional football career.

Of course, he was talented.

Of course, he was skilled.

Of course, he looked incredible in those skintight clothes and shoulder pads.

But what stood out above all those things, even how he looked in his sporting gear, was that he never, ever quit.

His team could be down thirty points from the other team, and he just became more ferocious, he dug in deeper, he never, ever gave up. That never-surrender, never-say-die attitude had pulled more than one impossible win from the hat.

His personal life was a different story.

He'd had a string of the most glamorous girlfriends in the world. Except for what appeared to her to be a humiliatingly public, disastrous choice in a first relationship, he'd never stuck long with anyone else.

More recently, she could see he'd gone underground. She understood perfectly how a man that well-known needed the refuge of a place like the *Seas du Jour.*

His own housekeeper had tossed him under the bus, exposed his private life in really unconscionable ways. That magazine issue had been devoted to him: "Catch of the Century."

It was ironic, really, that she ended up feeling sorry for him—the man who had, as she'd already seen on board his vessel, absolutely everything.

She went to shut the door.

But then she heard it.

Softly. A trick of the wind, perhaps.

"Marco."

Crazy to answer, and yet she did. "Polo."

"Marco." It came again, stronger.

There was no not recognizing the voice this time. She started to move toward it, but stopped.

He came. Marco Polo, running up the path toward her, crying his recognition and his welcome. He was dragging a leash behind him.

He wasn't really a kitten anymore, kind of at that gangly not-very-cute teenager stage. Still, she would have known him anywhere.

She crouched and held out her arms.

The cat leaped into them.

Then the call came again. "Marco."

She followed it. And there was Gage, behind the garden wall. She realized, too late, she was wearing a T-shirt with a stretched-out neck, shorts she slept in. She realized, too late, she didn't have on a speck of makeup and her hair had developed a funny green tinge from swimming in chlorinated pools.

But when Gage's eyes rested on her, it was apparent he didn't see any of that.

He only saw *her.*

"What are you doing?" she asked, taking him in hungrily. He was holding the empty cat carrier.

He thrust it at her. She saw it was not for a cat at all.

"I missed your birthday," he said. "I remembered the day, from your license."

She handed him Marco Polo and pried open the lid of the container. Her eyes smarted. Inside was the ugliest, most beautiful cake she had ever seen, with white icing and liberal candy sprinkles on top of it.

"Gage," she whispered.

"I'm drowning."

Of course that made no sense. They were a long way from the sea.

"There are so many ways for a man to drown," he told her softly. "So many. I need rescuing from the dark sea I find myself in."

She set down the cake. He set down the cat.His arms folded around her. She tilted back her head and looked into his glorious face.

She realized the utter silliness of everything she had done since she'd left him. How she had tried to become worthy, somehow, of love.

His love.

Because what she had always dreamed of seeing was already in his eyes.

She didn't have to earn it.

She didn't have to be worthy of it.

What she saw in his eyes accepted her exactly as she was. He had always seen her, even when she had lost sight of herself.

Maybe especially then.

"I need you," he said hoarsely, his lips touching her green hair. "I want you to give us a chance."

"Yes," she whispered back, and then stronger, "Yes."

The cat cried loudly and they looked down. Marco Polo had nudged the top farther off the container and had his face buried in the cake. He paused for a moment, looked at them and meowed. It sounded as if he'd said yes, too.

"There's just one condition," he whispered.

"And that is?"

"Please don't sing."

"But I've been taking lessons!"

"Yes, I heard. The entire neighborhood was slamming windows shut as I arrived."

"But I'm inspired by you!"

"By me?"

"I've been watching some of your career," she

admitted. "And if I've learned something from you, Gage, it's never give up."

"That's out of context," he said. "I've given up on lots of things I had no aptitude for. The trainer thought we should all take yoga one year. For improved flexibility." He snorted. "One class."

"Would it be a deal-breaker?" she asked. "If I sang?"

In answer, he picked her up and cradled her against his chest. "There are no deal-breakers," he told her softly, suddenly serious.

"Oh, good," she said. "Because you have not met my mother."

He ducked down without letting go of his hold of her and picked up the container. With Marco Polo following, he carried her up to the house, and she sang softly, the whole way, a love song to him.

EPILOGUE

THE STRANGEST THING of all, Gage thought, was how he had come to love her singing—those funny little warbles, not improved at all by lessons. He did not know how any teacher in good conscience could continue to take her money, but the man still did.

Maybe the teacher heard it, too, beyond the missed notes and the inability to hold a tune.

Because if a man listened with his heart, instead of his ears, all he could hear was the joy. Hailey's songs were like a celebration of each dawn, each day, each tiny miracle. Not that he would ever let her know. It was one of those insider jokes between them, guaranteed to bring a smile to her face when he covered his ears and pleaded with her to stop.

Her mother, of course, was another story.

Sheila Witherspoon was aggravating, self-centered and abrasive, a toxic cocktail made up of two main ingredients—victimhood and entitlement.

Still, in a few minutes, she would be his mother-in-law. He had accepted she was going to be the worst part of "for better or worse."

There she was, sitting beside his mom, dressed

in a flamboyant, low-cut, look-at-me dress that was the antithesis of his mother's worthy-of-the-queen pale pink suit and matching hat.

They would have barely said their "I do's" when she'd bolt outside for a cigarette.

But she was sober. For three weeks this time.

As he watched, his mother—who had looked at every single challenge in her life as an opportunity to give more and love deeper—took Hailey's mother's hand in her own and held it on her lap.

Reminding him how both Hailey and his mother constantly showed him that love accepted and healed and made everything better.

Love forgave Sheila for the fact she had not been and would never be mother of the year.

This was what love did: when he looked at his soon to be mother-in-law he saw that she had played a part in making the woman he loved.

The steel in her spine that had kept Hailey alive in the water that night came from this.

Her ability to be kind and compassionate and empathetic came from this.

Her love of those children who filled several rows of church pews had come from this. Those children, and their families, represented every single year she had taught, and their absolute devotion to Hailey shone in small, upturned faces.

Her ability to rise above, to find her core of inner strength, her sense of herself, had come from facing down the challenges of her childhood.

The music started—Mendelssohn's "Wedding March."

The back doors of the church squeaked open. But it was not the bride who came in first.

He'd had his doubts about this part, but if ever a cat could be trusted for the job, it was Marco Polo. He was more dog than cat. He followed them everywhere. He was a part of everything they did. He liked to ride in a backpack when they hiked or skied, and he loved the basket on motorcycles and bikes.

He had completely removed the fickle public's focus from Gage. Marco Polo's fan page had a million followers and counting. Unlike his owner—though the cat might have debated who owned whom—he lapped up the attention and affection.

Such was his popularity that the location of the wedding and Marco's role in it had been kept top secret, though they would reveal pictures—only of him, not of the bride and groom—onto his social media pages later for his hungry audience.

The famous cat, after hesitating just a moment to accept some much-deserved adoration from one of those children, appeared to, suddenly, remember his rehearsals.

He refocused and followed the little trail of cat treats up to the front of the church, gave a squeal of pure delight when he saw Gage and raced toward him.

He was intercepted by Mike, Gage's brother-in-law, who took off the wedding ring attached to the pillow with ribbons with an audible sigh of relief.

Mike had not been Gage's first choice for best man, but Seth had said no.

The door creaked open, again.

His niece came through, tossing flower petals enthusiastically. *See?* he wanted to tell his sister. He hadn't wasted the money on that Belle dress, after all. Sarah got to wear it again.

His sister arrived next, clutching her bouquet, unable to stanch the flow of tears as she came toward him.

Kate and Hailey were already family, closer than most sisters.

His sister's tears reminding him, poignantly, of the bonds of family. His and Hailey's joy was also Kate's joy. This was the moment she had dreamed of for him, well before he'd ever dreamed of it for himself.

And then, Hailey came in. He wasn't sure he'd ever seen a woman look quite so glorious, gliding toward him in a confection of white silk that was somehow pure innocence and sensuality combined. It hugged her bodice, skimmed her hips, hinted at some slender curves and accentuated others.

Seth, who had accepted her invitation instead of Gage's, was standing in for the father she had never known. His arm was looped through hers, and as they came toward him, Gage nodded his thanks to the strongest, most reliable man he had ever known.

The brother he had never had.

And then, he was stepping toward her, and she was stepping toward him. He took both her hands in his. He took in the lovely familiarity of her face, felt his heart swell with fulfillment.

The music stopped, and there was a sudden, expectant silence. He leaned in toward her and put his mouth very close to her ear.

"Don't sing," he whispered.

* * * * *

If you enjoyed this story,
check out these other great reads
from Cara Colter

Invitation to His Billion-Dollar Ball
Their Hawaiian Marriage Reunion
The Billionaire's Festive Reunion
Accidentally Engaged to the Billionaire

All available now!